Timothy
Tattercoat

Timothy Tattercoat

MARYEL *and* RONALD CHANEY

Illustrated by Garry MacKenzie

1 9 5 8

HOUGHTON MIFFLIN COMPANY BOSTON

The Riverside Press Cambridge

This book is affectionately dedicated to the beloved animals, both living and dead, whose antics and love made it possible; to animal shelters, large and small, throughout the world; and to the kind "human" people who enable them to exist.

CONTENTS

Timothy
Tattercoat

1

TIMOTHY TATTERCOAT *Himself*

THE MOST WONDERFUL THING about Timothy Tattercoat was that although his paint sometimes became chipped and faded his smile never did. It always remained the same throughout the years, wherever he might be, and the mischievous twinkle never left his bright, shining, jet-black glass eyes.

Timothy Tattercoat was a merry-go-round horse. Once he had stood on a huge round platform with twenty-six other merry-go-round horses. That was in the days of the big circus; gay, happy days, with Timothy turning and moving up and down to the luring music of the calliope, and happy children riding on his back. Then Timothy joined a small carnival that traveled about from place to place, visiting the children who lived too far away from the big circus.

Timothy had seen the world, or at least a great portion of it. And wherever he went he had brought magic, the magic of happiness.

When the carnival went out of business, Timothy Tattercoat was left in a deserted field along with other discarded, damaged goods. No one wanted him because one of his legs was broken. He was put in a junk yard and forgotten. The rain and weather faded and cracked his brightly painted coat. This seemed to be the end of Timothy, but still his eyes twinkled and his smile remained, because Timothy knew that the magic which lived inside his little wooden body would not desert him.

And he was right. One day a man came hunting for some iron bars and, in rummaging about, discovered Timothy.

"How much for this old merry-go-round horse?" he asked the junk dealer.

"Oh, a dollar, I reckon. He's been here for a long time. I need the space, so I'll be glad to get him out of the way."

"I think my little girl would like him. We could paint him and put him in our garden. One of his legs seems to be missing, though. I wonder if it can be located."

They dug around in the trash for almost an hour before the missing leg was discovered.

Then Timothy and his leg were hauled away in a wagon.

The wagon stopped beside a big white house surrounded by huge trees and a large, wonderful flower garden. If Timothy could, he would have whinnied with delight. At last he had a home. Someone wanted him. And from that moment on, he resolved that the special magic of happiness which was his would be used to help all the lost, homeless, unwanted creatures, such as he had been, that came his way.

He was lifted from the wagon and carried to a big, sweet-smelling barn. A small titian-haired girl came skipping into the barn.

"Oh, Daddy, a real merry-go-round horse!"

Timothy's heart swelled. A little girl. A child to make happy again. This was what merry-go-round horses were for.

"But, Daddy, isn't he kind of sad and tattered?"

Her father laughed. "He certainly is, Laurie. That is because he needs to be painted. Since he is yours, I thought you would like to decide what color to paint him."

Laurie studied the faded horse for a long time.

"I like gray horses with black spots, and silvery-white manes and tails," she said at last. "I think I have a name for him too. I'm going to call him Tattercoat. He should have a first name, though. But what sounds nice with Tattercoat?" she puzzled.

High above her in a live oak a catbird called gaily, *Timee, timee-ee.*

"Timmy, that's it," cried Laurie. "Timothy Tattercoat."

Timothy's broken leg was glued in place and tied securely for several days. Then his shabby old coat was peeled down to the very quick and sandpapered until not a bubble or crack remained. Next a coat of gray paint was put on, and after it dried, a second and a third.

Laurie watched each step with enthusiasm. And watching with equal interest was the nine-year-old boy from next door, Lance O'Leary. When Timothy was ready they came to the barn together, with new paint brushes in their hands, and carefully put on each shining black splotch. Next they painted the grinning open mouth and lips with red, and made the big teeth dazzling white. And finally they washed the last bit of dust from Timothy's black glass eyes until they shone like stars. How they twinkled!

Timothy was placed on a pedestal right in the center of the garden. Magnolia and mimosa trees blossomed high above him, and roses and jasmine flowered at his feet, making his entire world smell like a heaven.

Timothy liked this better than even the circus and carnival days. There he had been only one of many merry-go-round horses, but here he was the only one and so very important, monarch of the garden and of the hearts of Laurie and Lance.

There were dogs, too. A big one, Lassie, part shepherd and part collie; beautiful Tippie, a thoroughbred collie; and Mack, Mr. MacGregor's hunting dog, who was so gun-shy he couldn't be used for hunting. There were puppies, of course, and in the big stable horses and colts and foals. There were kittens, and a tame bullfrog who lived in the lily pool. And once there was a little pig, but he grew so big that he had to be moved to a larger farm where there was more room. And always there were birds building nests in the trees and singing in the honeysuckle.

Timothy felt that it was the happiest place in the world.

Laurie and Lance made up wonderful stories in which Timothy Tattercoat was always the hero rising from his pedestal and whizzing through the night on magical journeys of his own.

But if they rushed to the window to look at the garden he would still be there, standing firmly on his pedestal. Well, they reasoned, he was magic, and could return to the garden in the twinkling of an eye.

Ronnie thought about Timothy Tattercoat's magic

as he lay awake in his upper berth listening to the wheels of the train speeding across the plains. Sometimes though, he knew, things happened over which even a merry-go-round horse's magic had no control. He had heard Timothy's story from Mother so many times that he felt it was his story too; how Lance went with his family to far-off Africa; how Mother had moved away from the big white house and they had lost track of each other. Then Ronnie dimly remembered a small house with Timothy Tattercoat proudly standing in a smaller garden, and a father who laughed and gaily tossed Ronnie into the air. And when Father did not come back from the war, there was a small apartment in Chicago hardly big enough for Ronnie and Mother and Bugs and Mitzi. The first time Ronnie really remembered Timothy was when he saw him in a stall-like box in a big warehouse. He looked faded and woebegone between the slats of his crate, all except his twinkling jet-black eyes and broad grin. Mother promised then that someday they would have room for Timothy. But it seemed as if Timothy decided to take things in his own hands and start using his magic again. How else could anybody account for that afternoon in the Natural History Museum, and the events that followed? Ronnie and Mother had been almost ready to leave when Ronnie stopped to watch a man sitting at an easel, painting a picture of the African lions. The man smiled at Ronnie, and then looked at Mother. He jumped to his feet, forgetting all about the wet painting, which toppled to the floor along with all the other equipment.

"Laurie . . . Laurie MacGregor!" the man cried.

"Lance O'Leary!"

Then everyone was all cluttered up together, laughing and crying at the same time, looking at each other and smiling happily.

And now three weeks later Ronnie and Mother and his new daddy were on a train westward to Daddy's home in the middle of a big game preserve high in the Rocky Mountains, where he lived and painted wild-life pictures for books and magazines. Daddy had said it was a place where there was plenty of room for Timothy Tattercoat, and acres and acres for Bugs and Mitzi to romp and play in. Bugs and Mitzi were an important part of the family and couldn't be left behind. Bugs was a toy poodle, snow-white with black eyes and nose. She weighed three pounds before she was clipped. Ronnie and Mother thought she was a spoiled dog, always trying to find some way to get people to pay attention to her, but they loved her, and Mitzi too. Mitzi was her daughter, and only part toy poodle. The other part was all kinds of nice dogs. She had black eyes and a black nose too, and her long silky hair was the color of honey.

Ronnie had worried a bit about leaving his friends at the Trailside Museum, where he often went to visit the abandoned animals, just a few blocks from the apartment. Raffles, the crippled raccoon, was his very special friend. But Daddy told him about all the wild animals in the forest and even mentioned that they would have their own Trailside Museum.

And best of all, Timothy Tattercoat would have his own garden again, a garden that looked out on high mountain peaks and rushing rivers and streams, and lots and lots of animals.

The wheels sang *Timothy ... Timothy ... Timothy Tattercoat* over and over again until Ronnie was sung to sleep.

2

TRADER HORN

THEY LEFT the city and wended their way up into the foothills and were soon deep in the heart of the Rocky Mountains. The air grew crisper and colder and thinner. Deep snow covered the high mountains, and above the mountain line still higher peaks sparkled in the sun.

They drove for over two hours before they turned off onto a side road which Daddy told Ronnie was on their property. Everywhere were signs which read NO HUNTING, NO GUNS ALLOWED, GAME PRESERVE, and BEWARE OF FOREST FIRES — BE SURE YOUR FIRE AND CIGARETTE ARE OUT!

Nestling among the mountains, which swept away into beyond, sat a long, low gray house. It was almost hidden by the snow, the big pine trees, and smaller silver, blue-and-green spruce trees.

This was home.

A medium-sized dog, tawny golden in color, and one

of the most beautiful Ronnie had ever seen, bounded forward to meet them. She was Penny, Daddy's dog. Not a thoroughbred, he said, except at heart.

As Mitzi's family climbed from the car she stood waiting politely to see what they wanted her to do. Mitzi was always polite. Bugs didn't care what anybody wanted her to do. She did what she wanted to. She took off through the snow and disappeared from view. This was her favorite game. She would let someone almost touch her, then like a shot bound away again, out of reach.

"Oh, the wild animals will surely get her!" Mother cried.

"There are no dangerous ones in the daytime, so near the house." Daddy smiled.

They started for the house. Bugs had ceased to be the center of attraction. Bewildered, she looked after the disappearing figures. This had never happened before. Usually she could keep someone chasing her for hours, through traffic, or through the park. It wasn't any fun unless her family were worried about her. Ordinarily she wouldn't give up this easily, but she was cold, her blue sweater was soggy with snow, and the high altitude made her feel strange, so she turned and followed them home through the drifts. When the door opened she was the first one inside.

The house was cool. Daddy scurried about, building fires in all five of the fireplaces. Even the kitchen, the largest and homiest room in the house, had a fireplace.

They were unpacking and hanging their clothing in the closets when they heard a big truck lumbering up the road. Everyone left unpacking and ran to help lift Timothy Tattercoat from the truck.

They put his crate in the barn, but he looked so pathetic that they knocked the slats away and stood him in the corner. Daddy said that they would repaint his tattered coat tomorrow.

Mother put on her blue jeans and began struggling with the little old iron cookstove. She couldn't make the fire burn, no matter how she tried. But Daddy could. He had it going in only a minute.

Suddenly there was laughter and shouting voices outside. The neighbors had come to welcome Lance O'Leary's new family.

There was a boy of twelve named Ralph, whose father owned the sawmill down the road. There was Elsa Pittman, a flaxen-haired girl, eight years old, just Ronnie's age, who had three brothers and two sisters. Then there was a big, twinkling-eyed man, named Mr. Mallow, who was a forest ranger. The Gale family was there, and several other families. Miss Gale taught at the one-room schoolhouse where Ronnie was to go to school. They had brought all kinds of good-tasting things to eat. It was a wonderful party.

That night Ronnie looked from his bedroom window under the eaves of the house. Around him stretched the forest. He saw some deer nibbling at bales of hay in the clearing. Far away, he heard two wolves, hunting and howling at the winter moon. But inside all was quiet and cozy, with Penny snuggled up beside Mitzi at the foot of his bed, and Bugs tormenting to be put underneath the covers.

"How will we collect animals for our Trailside Museum, Daddy?" Ronnie asked at breakfast the next morning.

"Oh, people drop animals from cars along the highway, and some of the wild ones wander down. We'll find them, don't worry," Daddy said confidently.

They went out to the barn, paintbrushes in hand, to paint Timothy Tattercoat. Ronnie took some clean rags, a stiff brush, and a bucket of hot soapy water to wash him first. When he reached Timothy's head his heart took a sickening tumble. One of his bright jet-glass eyes was gone. Ronnie knew that both eyes had been there when they left him in the barn the night before. He had looked him over carefully.

He called Daddy and pointed to the empty socket.

Daddy looked and then walked over to the opposite corner of the barn. He moved a board leaning there and reached inside a nest of twigs, sticks, and rags. He took a number of things from the nest — bright beads, glass, pebbles, a thimble, a tarnished sheriff's badge — and finally emerged with the missing eye.

"Daddy, you're magic! How did you know it was there?" Ronnie cried.

"Anything that is missing around this place is bound to be there," he laughed.

A beautiful, sleek dark brown and white rat came

out of the nest, looked at Daddy, and sat down be-
seechingly on his foot.

"This is Trader Horn," said Daddy, patting the rat.
"He's a pack rat, or a trade rat. Once when I returned
from a trip to the Painted Desert I found him huddled
in the back of the station wagon inside my bedding,
clutching his sheriff's badge. He had decided to move
and had brought his most cherished possession, the
badge which he had found on the desert, lost, no
doubt, on some long forgotten manhunt. I put him in
the barn, never dreaming that he'd stay. But he did.
He has built a nest here and scoured the area for new
treasures to put in it. He has ways of getting inside the
house, which I can't discover. He often takes treasures
from there, but since he is a trade rat, he always leaves
something in place of the things he takes. Although he
steals, he is not dishonest, for to him it is an even
exchange. I named him for the famous trader, Trader
Horn. Isn't he a pretty fellow? Clean, intelligent,
and friendly — something like a squirrel. Evidently
he found Timothy's eye loose and took it home with
him. If you look on the floor near Timothy, you'll discover whatever it is he has left in place of the eye."

Ronnie looked. There lay a bright rosy pebble.

"Do you mean he's ours?"

"He certainly is. Although I suppose many people

would call him a pest, I'm very fond of Trader Horn. He is a cunning, entertaining fellow."

"Well, we already have the beginning of our Trailside Museum then, haven't we?"

"Yes, I suppose we have. We have three dogs and a pack rat. But Ronnie, whatever we have in our Trailside Museum can never be caged. We do not want to keep anything against its will. And then, too, it is against the law to pen wild creatures here on a game preserve."

"That's all right with me. Cages are sad. I think I like animals running wild and free, just staying because they like us."

Timothy's eye was glued in place securely and he was given his first coat of paint. Then a second, with particular attention to the black spots. Last of all he was given a clear coat of preservative because he would be standing outside in all kinds of weather. He looked elegant, but he couldn't be put outside yet because the snow and frozen ground made it impossible to pour cement for his pedestal.

Ronnie had tried to tell Mother about Trader Horn, but she had been busy and hadn't paid much attention. She had been struggling with the old iron cookstove, which she had christened the "Iron Maiden," because like that ancient instrument of torture it caused untold anguish and misery, both to her disposition and her hands and arms that were covered with burns. So she hadn't paid much attention to what Ronnie had said about Trader Horn. If she had, she wouldn't have been so startled a few days later when she met him.

She came into the kitchen, her arms loaded with groceries, and let out a shriek when she saw Trader Horn marching across the drainboard.

"A rat!" she gasped, dropping the sacks on the floor, "A big, live rat, right here in our kitchen."

"Oh, honey," Daddy said, "don't scream so. You'll frighten him half to death. That is no ordinary rat. He is Trader Horn, a trade rat."

"I don't care what his name is. You chase him out of here."

"He came to trade. He's harmless. He just wants to be friends."

"Well, I don't want to be friends. I just want you to get him out of here. Stop up the holes, so he can't get in."

"I can't find them," Daddy said patiently. "Now honey, don't carry on so. You should have met him before. He's a member of the household."

"What is that he's taking with him?" Mother pointed. "It's one of my new sewing machine attachments. And, of all things, he's left a pine cone."

"Yes, those shining sewing machine attachments would fascinate him. You'll have to keep them hidden in a drawer. And you will have to keep your jewelry locked up. He will love that. But don't worry, he will always leave something in its place."

"You mean every time I want to sew, I'll have to dig my attachments out of his nest? Every time I want to dress, I'll have to hunt my jewelry out of the barn?"

"I guess so," Daddy said. "I'm always having to retrieve my fountain pen and pencil from there. But don't ever remove the things from his nest without leaving something instead. That would hurt his feelings, and he wouldn't think we were being honest, and maybe he would leave."

"That's just what I want him to do," Mother said unfeelingly.

"When you know him better, you won't feel that way. He is one of the cleanest fellows imaginable, and well worth his keep. There is not a single bug in the barn since he has come here to live. He keeps them killed off."

Trader Horn looked about at the confusion he had

caused, his black pop-eyes bewildered. He laid the
sewing machine attachment on the drainboard, and
rubbed his little white vest, his long whiskers standing
straight out at the sides of his pointed nose.

"Now you watch how he gets out," Mother ordered,
"then we'll know how he gets in and can stop up the
places."

They started picking up the groceries from the floor.
When they looked around, Trader Horn had completely disappeared — the sewing machine attachment
along with him.

3

TATTERCOAT RANGE

Do you think the ground has thawed enough, Daddy?" Ronnie didn't have to say for what. Everyone knew. He meant thawed enough to pour cement for Timothy Tattercoat's pedestal.

"Goodness, no," Daddy replied. "Look how hard it is. You couldn't dig it out with an ax. Even the chipmunks are still sleeping. You were wondering the other day why you hadn't seen any chipmunks. You won't until spring, and then this will be one of the busiest spots in the forest."

They had walked to a clearing a mile above the house where a big chipmunk village lay in deep pine-needle loam beneath the ice and snow.

"The chipmunks have all hibernated for the winter, like the bears. They roll themselves into tiny striped balls, beneath the roots and earth, and sleep until spring awakens them. During this long sleep they do not feel hunger or cold, or anything at all. Naturalists say this sleep is almost like an anesthetic, that a leg could be cut off and the animal would never feel it, and that hardly any blood would flow. Chipmunks are the gayest little fellows in the forest. There is a pet one named Scamper who lives in a hole beside the big stone fence down by the gate. Before too long you will see him."

Lance O'Leary was an expert woodsman and naturalist himself. That was one of the reasons he was a nature illustrator. He knew practically all there was to know about animals and the forest. There were no tracks on the range or the mountains that he didn't recognize.

Not far from the house he had pointed out a heavy branch on one of the spruce trees. To Ronnie it looked little different from the rest. But he learned that it was the nest of a spruce squirrel, who cunningly builds his home of broken spruce twigs, interweaving them among the living branches until they all look the same, except that the nests are thicker and heavier. Even experienced woodsmen had difficulty discovering these nests.

Daddy knew exactly why the snowshoe rabbits had such funny big feet, and why they turned white all over in winter to match the snow, and brown again at other seasons. He explained that because a rabbit is prey to so many larger creatures nature had given

him certain ways to protect himself. His color changing with the seasons made him difficult to see; and in
the winter he grew furry snowshoes that enabled him
to skim across snow which would bog down other
creatures. When he no longer needed his white coat
and furry snowshoes, they disappeared, leaving his feet
looking like any rabbit's, and his coat turned brown
again to match the surroundings.

Ronnie realized that every creature which lives has
its own definite purpose in the scheme of things. Even
the small coyote, once despised and hunted by men,
kept down destructive rabbits and other vermin that
caused more harm on the ranches and farms than the
coyote did. Some of the ranchers were even having
coyotes brought back into the area and offering them
protection.

"Are there any coyotes on our land?" he asked.

"There surely are. Keep your eyes open and you
will see them. There is one who is a sort of pet. I
rescued him during a flood when he was a pup stranded
on a log in the middle of the river."

"Why," Ronnie said excitedly, "we certainly do
have a Trailside Museum."

"Yes, I guess we have," smiled Daddy.

Near the hidden chipmunk village, in an icebound
dell, were several deer. One young doe came up

and nuzzled in the pocket of Daddy's big coat for an apple, a carrot or a lump of sugar. She was a pet named Lady. Daddy had fed and cared for her since she was born.

There was hay in the dell and a white, hard surface — a salt lick which had been placed there for the deer. Ronnie had seen airplanes flying over the mountains, dropping big bundles of hay into the timberlands. He had been curious and learned it was the only way stock and game could get food in the severe winter weather. The Forestry Department, or Daddy and the other ranchers, would furnish the hay and arrange for it to be flown over the barren land. Before this food had been brought to them the hungry deer had torn away the lower branches and trunks of all the aspen trees in the area.

Airplanes were used in other emergencies as well. Daddy told about one time a sweeping forest fire, the most dreaded thing that can happen in a forest, destroyed all the beavers in the upper regions. Without the industrious beavers to build dams and conserve the soil and water, streams had flooded and cut into the land, washing away vast amounts of good earth. Healthy beavers from other areas had been put in small bags and dropped by tiny parachutes onto the devastated land to begin rebuilding.

They paused and Daddy pointed to some tracks in the snow. "Ronnie, do you notice anything peculiar about these tracks?

"Those are wolf tracks," he went on. "Two of them are hunting this area together, a big one and his smaller mate. See the track of the left forefoot? That is the track of a very special fellow. He is a giant of a wolf, Ole Cripple Toe. You can see by the track that one of his toes is missing. He is a very crafty old one, and I can't remember the time when he wasn't in these forests. Government hunters who are sent in to trap an area that becomes overrun with wolves had tried to get Ole Cripple Toe, but he is almost ghostlike in the way he strikes and vanishes. In fact, I have come upon his tracks as far as thirty miles away. I have grown fond of him. As long as he stays up here and does not come down farther on the range, I shall never harm him but will let him go his wild way in peace. I admire him for his intelligence and wisdom, and like to hear his cry on winter nights."

"I like this place," Ronnie said softly. "I think it should have a name, though. It seems that everyone's home should have a name."

"I think so, too," Daddy answered as they started homeward. "What do you think we should name it?"

"Well, I've been thinking about it a lot. I think we

should call it Tattercoat Range, in honor of Timothy Tattercoat."

"That is a splendid name," Daddy agreed. "As soon as we set up Timothy you and Mother can plant a garden around him, and we will officially christen our home 'Tattercoat Range.'"

A few weeks later, getting off the school bus, Ronnie started up the little lane toward home and suddenly froze in his tracks. The world was alive with bluebirds. They made the sky seem bluer and the meadow blossomed with the little creatures. Thousands and thousands of bluebirds were in the trees and on the land of Tattercoat Range. They had come back from their winter vacation in the South. Wherever bluebirds come, it is said, they bring happiness. And here they were on Tattercoat Range. It was a wonderful sight. Soon they would be building their nests, laying eggs, and raising their children, two broods each spring season. And the curious, happy thing about the bluebirds was their loving home life. The older of the two broods, having learned to fly before the arrival of the second, would help to raise the newer ones, just as older brothers and sisters do.

When Ronnie looked down from the sky and over at the big stone fence post he saw a lone chipmunk sitting there. Scamper, the eagerly awaited pet chip-munk, had awakened from his long sleep. He was look-ing about him with bright black eyes for something to fill his empty stomach. Ronnie moved slowly forward, his hand rummaging inside his school lunch box for bread crusts. Scamper didn't run away. He was ac-customed to being fed in this spot. And now, very hungry after his long winter, he waited for scraps.

He stuffed the crusts into his cheek pouches with tiny hands. Then he sat up straight on his hind legs, his forefeet clutching a scrap that wouldn't fit into his pouch, as if saying thank you. A greedy bluejay swooped down for the remaining scraps, and only then did Scamper dart away with almost the speed of light into the hole beside the post.

Ronnie ran all the rest of the way home to tell Mother and Daddy that the bluebirds had come back, and that the chipmunks were beginning to come out of hibernation, and what a very busy forest this was beginning to be.

Before the gray house he stopped.

Timothy Tattercoat was no longer in the barn. He was leaning against a silver-spruce tree, a bluebird perched on his shoulder. And there in the very center where the garden was to be Daddy had dug a hole and was pouring cement.

4

RAFFLES, *the Raccoon*

As soon as Timothy Tattercoat was set in elegant splendor in the garden as overlord of Tattercoat Range all kinds of magical, wonderful things began to happen. Maybe they would have happened anyway, but one could never be sure.

First of all, the chipmunks near the house, in the forest, and at the big chipmunk village near the deer's salt lick came out and made the woodlands happy with their antics. They were like little clowns. Then the bluebirds built their nests, and over the entire range hundreds of tiny creatures came into the world, opening their eyes for the very first time. Bears came out of hibernation from overturned trees and from the caves on distant slopes. Tagging along beside each fussy mother bear were the babies who had been born while she had been deep in sleep. Such fuzzy, eager little cubs they were; so full of mischief and fun. Nothing seemed to bother them at all. They fished and tumbled and played, dug for grubs and ants; being both flesh and plant eaters, they could always find food except in the winter when they did not need it. None of the brown or black bears became pets, but they became friends of sorts because they made the forest more interesting with their activities.

Along about the time the first bear came from hibernation, with two tiny cubs toddling along beside her, Timothy Tattercoat's garden took form. Daddy transplanted more small spruce trees from the forest, setting them among those already there. He and Mother and Ronnie went to a little mountain valley where the orchid-blue wild iris grew and brought back bushel baskets of the bulbs to be put in the earth along with columbine plants and other wild flowers. Many varieties of seeds were planted, and the neighbors brought choice plants from their various gardens. All that was left to do now was sit back and watch Timothy Tattercoat's garden grow and blossom.

The dogs were an important part of Tattercoat Range too, each with a different personality. Bugs was so cute and bad, so endearing with her little tricks such as walking around on her hind legs and patting her forefeet as though she were clapping her hands. Her crowning achievement was trying to crow like a rooster. Of course, she didn't really crow, but did make a howl that sounded a little like a rooster's crow. Whereupon she would be so pleased with herself and the attention she received that she wouldn't stop. And then there was Mitzi, who spent her entire life trying to please her family. She wanted to mother everything, even the tiny wood mice and the little birds. Penny was exceptionally smart. Daddy had taught her many tricks when they had had so much time together before Mother and Ronnie came. She had learned to climb a ladder and turn on the lights, jumping up and pull-

ing the long chains that hung from overhead. One dark, dismal day, they had all returned from the general store to find every light in the house blazing away. Evidently Penny had grown bored alone in the dark house.

Mother was learning a lot too. She had reached the point where Trader Horn no longer terrified her. She grumbled very little when she had to dig things out of his nest, leaving a ten-cent strand of beads or something in their place, even apologizing to Trader Horn for having to take back her own jewelry. Yes, Mother was adjusting. But she didn't want any more pets. She said they had enough and that there wasn't room for another single one.

Mother, however, had reckoned without the special magic of Tattercoat Range.

One sunny day after school Ralph invited Ronnie to go home with him. Before they started for the barn his mother gave them polished apples and fresh doughnuts. Ralph had a wonderful family. His older brother was studying to be a veterinarian and usually had wounded or sick animals being treated in the barn. His father, who owned the sawmill, let them dig caves or jump and slide in the huge piles of sawdust. It was fun too, to watch Shep, Ralph's shepherd dog, scatter rats and mice out of the nests they had made in the sawdust.

"Ronnie, come here, I want to show you something," Ralph said, leaning over a box in the corner of the barn.

Ronnie peered inside. Huddled down inside the box, close together, staring at the boys with round, shining eyes, were two tiny coons.

Ronnie forgot all about the piles of sawdust.

"Oh!" he gasped. "Baby coons — lucky you! At Trailside Museum there was a big one, named Raffles. He was just about the best friend I had in Chicago. I visited him every Saturday, and the last day I was there I took him a string of blue beads to remember me by. He hung them around his neck and looked at himself in the drinking water. Where did you get these? They are the nicest little things."

"They fell out of their nest when my father was chopping down a big tree so he gave them to me. Do you want one? You can take your pick," Ralph said generously.

"Oh, boy! Can I?"

Ronnie picked up one of the wee furry animals and huddled it against him. Its tiny black hands were almost human. It looked as if it were wearing a black mask around its shining eyes, and it had the fattest, fluffiest ringed tail. The little animal bit him, but not enough to hurt.

"I'm going to name it Raffles, in honor of my friend at Trailside."

"Are you sure your mother won't mind? She's a city woman, you know, and city women are kind of peculiar."

"Not my mother. She's not a bit peculiar. She doesn't care what we bring home. She says she does and fusses for a little while. But she just pretends. She really likes all of our animals."

"You want a box to carry him in?"

"No. He would get cold," said Ronnie. "I'll carry him in my pocket."

"Well, you'd better button it down, for coons have very handy hands. Their real name is raccoon, you know — at least that's what city folks call them."

"Shucks, I know that, but we woodsmen don't ever call them anything except coons."

Shep danced around, nosing at Ronnie's pocket as they went through the gate.

Halfway down the logging road, he thought of his manners.

He turned and yelled back, "I had a swell time. Come to see me. And thanks for the coon."

When he burst into the kitchen, Mother was at the Iron Maiden, preparing dinner. Daddy was building something which looked like a big straw-lined drawer into the kitchen fireplace wall.

"Hello, Ronnie," he said, looking up from his work. "I'm building an orphan box."

"An orphan box? You mean a box to put money in for the orphans?"

"Not money — orphans. This will be much handier than keeping boxes sitting around everyplace for all of your little orphan birds and animals."

The last thing Ronnie had brought home had been a poor blind bluejay. But it had died, and now there was nothing in any of the small boxes scattered around the kitchen.

Ronnie pulled out the orphan box, admired it, and pushed it back again. There were funny little animals painted all over it. It stood about two feet from the floor and could be pulled out and pushed back so that the little occupants couldn't fall out or get stepped on.

"Wait until you see what I've got!" he said, reaching into his squirming pocket. "The orphan box won't have to look so lonely and empty."

"Ronald!" That was the name Mother always reserved for emergencies. "Don't tell me you've brought another animal home. We haven't room for another thing."

"Then why is Daddy building an orphan box?" Ronnie asked reasonably.

"Whatever it is," said Mother, ignoring his last remark, "you just take it back where you found it."

"I didn't find it. Ralph gave it to me. And it isn't nice to take things back that folks give you." Ronnie brought the little coon out of his pocket.

"Oh," cried Mother, just as Ronnie had known she would do. "Isn't it just darling?" Once mother saw something, the battle was half won.

"May I keep him, Mother? You said I could have a kind of Trailside Museum."

"Yes, but I meant beside the trail, not inside the house. But I guess it will be all right this time. However, don't bring another thing home. We simply haven't a bit more room."

"Not even if it's something that has fallen from its nest, or is blind, or starving, or hurt?"

"Well — in cases such as those — " said Mother, who would have brought those things home herself.

Daddy pulled out the orphan box and helped Ronnie fit the little coon into it.

Raffles showed no real fear of the dogs who, after

walking about stiff-legged and sniffing, had left him alone, except for Mitzi who started mothering him from the moment she saw him.

The first night the little coon cried and whimpered like a puppy, probably because he missed his twin, so Mother said that he could stay in the orphan box for tonight, but after this he would have to go to the barn, because whoever heard of a coon in the house?

The next morning Raffles had a bath, for he still carried the strong odor of his wood nest. After the bath they put him back in the box, now lined with clean straw, so that he would not catch pneumonia in the drafty barn. Just for today he could stay inside. The next day was cool and rainy, and Raffles still couldn't be moved to the drafty barn or woodshed. After that, everyone sort of forgot that the orphan box was supposed to be only temporary quarters, and there he lived until he outgrew it, sometimes sharing it with other, newer orphans.

Raffles learned to climb out of his box, first putting his monkey-like hands over the edge and his big eyes peering out from his black mask. The dogs were usually lying in the kitchen, noses pointed toward Raffles, their eyes on the box. They would rouse and prick their ears when he moved about, but they didn't bother him. At first he would climb back into his box, knowing he was safe there. But there came a time when he seemed to think that he was a dog too and would run and play with the rest.

Feeding him was no problem because he liked so many things to eat, but eggs were his favorite food. It disgruntled the dogs no end when Raffles washed his food in their pan of drinking water. He had one of his own right beside it. But he did it all the time. It didn't do any good to slap him for spoiling the dogs' drinking water. He just slapped right back.

"Do you know why a coon washes its food before eating it, Ronnie?" Daddy asked, sketching a picture of Raffles.

"All coons do that. Because they want their food to be clean, I guess."

"Partly. But the real reason is because raccoons do not have much saliva, and in order to swallow their food they have to wet it enough to be moist."

"Imagine a tiny baby coon like Raffles being smart enough to know that."

"Well, coons are intelligent certainly, but moistening their food is instinct. All animals have particular instincts — and sometimes, people do too," he added, grinning.

Ralph and Ronnie had a contest to see whose little coon could learn the most tricks, but when Raffles learned to play ball and hold a tiny book in his paws and turn the pages, Ralph was forced to concede Raffles was smarter.

5

FILBERT, *the Nutty Cat*

PENNY AND MITZI walked with Ronnie every morning to the highway where he got the school bus. Sometimes Bugs would go if the notion suited her and there wasn't something else she would rather do. After Ronnie got on the bus, the dogs would turn and trot back up the little road toward home, chasing each other and the birds running around on the ground. When they made a leap the birds would fly up into the branches of the trees and scold from their lofty perches. The pine jays in particular seemed to know that this was just a game, and would dart at the dogs, almost touching them, then fly a little farther along and do the same thing all over again. The jays never left Tattercoat Range, but remained throughout the year, robbing, squalling, pestering, and beautiful. Although they are considered the biggest robbers of the timberland, they repay their victims by policing the forest, screaming warning cries when danger, real or fancied, approaches.

Whenever the dogs saw a squirrel run up a tree they would spend hours watching for its reappearance. They never forgot which tree it was, and every time they passed it they would look up hopefully. This kept them pretty busy, because there were so many squirrels, and so very many trees. And the chipmunks kept them busy too.

There was one word that each dog was taught to know and obey. That was the word "stop." Daddy patiently taught them, and even Raffles learned it. Bugs was the only one who ever disobeyed, and then to escape the punishment she knew was forthcoming she would run and hide someplace, such as in the laundry bag. But even she gradually learned the reason for such commands. One time when Daddy had said, "Stop, Bugs! Stop, Mitzi and Penny!" Bugs kept right on going and fell through the icy crust of a cold mountain stream. She certainly was glad when Daddy dragged her out, dried her off, and put her in his warm pocket. Bugs would never do anything anyone wanted her to do. Mother made excuses for her, saying that she probably had reasons which, to her, were good ones. As a matter of fact she sometimes had. The other dogs would join gaily in ball games with Raffles, who climbed onto something high and threw the ball for them to retrieve. But not Bugs. One time when she had played the ball had rolled into the hot ashes of the fireplace. Bugs ran to pick it up, but the ball stuck to her mouth and burned her tongue, so she never retrieved again.

"We have such a lovely family," Mother said, "the animal members as well as the human, that we just couldn't possibly do without any one of them. But really, we haven't room for any more, so don't even consider another pet."

Daddy winked at Ronnie and said all right.

But of all people, it was Mother who was the next offender.

She said that she wanted to raise a few chickens, just enough to supply them with eggs and to furnish a fryer now and then. Daddy agreed, and said that one could hardly consider a few chickens as pets.

But that was before they met Mother's chickens.

Shirley, Myrna, Heddy, and Jimmy Cagney were the first. They were little black bantams, with feathers growing down over their yellow feet like chaps. Their names suited their individual personalities. Of course, they all became pets. So Mother said they would have to get a few more chickens, just plain, ordinary ones which couldn't possibly be pets. She bought a few red hens, and a big ferocious rooster who made life miserable for everyone, especially plucky little Jimmy Cagney. But no one could eat those either.

Then came the fatal day when Mother decided to drive up to visit Mrs. Drake, since Daddy would be at the salt lick all day getting pictures of the deer.

After school Ronnie was making himself a peanut butter and jelly sandwich, getting lots of help from Raffles, when Mother came in with a shoe box under her arm. She put the box on the floor and opened it. A half-grown kitten jumped out and the dogs rushed gleefully forward. The kitten took one look at them and at his strange surroundings, arched his back, and started spitting at them. Looking about for some means of escape, he ran like a streak across the living room to the fireplace, the dogs barking furiously at his heels.

Mother tried to hold the dogs and Ronnie yelled *stop* until he nearly burst. But this time they didn't stop. The kitten ran across the ashes, up the rough stones and inside the chimney.

Ronnie tried to coax him back, but only succeeded in getting covered with soot. The cat refused to come down.

Mother said, "Oh, if only Daddy were here to help."

Ronnie said, "If he had been here, it wouldn't have

happened because the dogs would have stopped when he told them to, and he wouldn't have let the fire go out."

"Let's go outside and maybe the cat will come down," Mother said.

Ronnie reached for Raffles, who was busy with both hands in the jelly jar. He and the dogs were banished from the house.

They walked over the crest of the hill and Ronnie threw pine cones for the dogs to chase, until it got so cool they had to go back. They fastened the outraged animals in the woodshed and went into the house.

Daddy had come home. Ronnie stared at him in horror.

"What are you doing?" he asked idiotically, for anyone could see what Daddy was doing.

"I'm building a fire in the fireplace," he replied reasonably, striking a match.

"Oh, no!" cried Ronnie. "There's a cat up the chimney."

"A cat!" Daddy yelled.

So the story had to be told.

"Well, there's only one thing to be done. It's too dark now to see up the chimney, so we will have to go up on the roof and poke him down."

Ronnie stayed by the fireplace to catch the cat, while Daddy went up on the icy roof and poked. All that came down was more soot, covering everything in the vicinity of the fireplace.

Mother went out into the kitchen for newspapers to catch the soot.

"Oh, Lance," she called timidly, "come on down. The cat is under the Iron Maiden. He must have come down while we were outside."

"You and your cat!" said Daddy, while he and Ronnie struggled to remove the soot from their eyes and faces. "There will be no more pets around this house — I heard you say it myself."

Mother was apologetic. "I know it, but I just couldn't refuse and hurt Mrs. Drake's feelings. She has been so nice to us. Maybe the cat will run away, or something," she added hopefully.

The half-grown gray kitten had completed his grooming beneath the stove. Each soft hair was polished. No soot remained on him.

Meow, he said as he lapped his saucer of milk, forgiving them for everything.

"He really is a beautiful cat," Mother said wistfully. "Just look at that long, silky smoke-gray hair."

"Smoke!" snorted Daddy. "If it had been anything

but a cat!" Evidently Daddy didn't want a cat, particularly this one.

"His ears have long hair in them. They are tufted, like the ears of a lynx. Maybe sometime you will need a cat model for your illustrations," Mother continued.

Daddy rebuilt the fire, saying that this was positively the last time the fire was going to be allowed to go out. One by one the dogs were let in to get used to the cat, but he crawled beneath the stove where they couldn't reach him and growled from his pearl-gray throat.

"Where is Raffles?" Ronnie asked after supper.

"He must still be in the woodshed," Mother said.

Ronnie looked everywhere in the woodshed, and called and whistled, but Raffles had gone.

Ronnie was inconsolable. "Raffles has run away. If he stays in the wilds, his collar will get too tight for him when he grows, and choke him to death."

Everybody felt badly.

The cat came warily from beneath the stove, wondering at his reception. These people had brought him here and seemed as if they wanted him. But from the minute he had come into this strange house, they seemed to have changed their minds.

Ronnie stroked the soft fur. He was a beautiful kitten, all right, but he wasn't Raffles.

The cat was made comfortable in the kitchen and they all went to bed.

In the middle of the night they were awakened by strange noises — *clatter, clatter, thump, thud, thump*.

Daddy went down in his bare feet to investigate. Suddenly there was a terrible crashing noise, accompanied by angry howls from Daddy. It sounded as if the entire rear end of the house were being demolished.

Mother and Ronnie jumped from their beds and ran down to see what was going on.

Daddy was sitting in the center of the floor. "It's your cat," he howled. "He found the sack of filbert nuts and was rolling them all over the kitchen floor. I stepped on them and nearly broke my neck."

But it wasn't his neck he was rubbing.

Mother sighed and kissed him. She looked as though she was having a terrible struggle to keep from laughing. But she didn't dare laugh.

"Believe me, I know just how you feel," she sympathized.

"No, you don't. Not in the same places anyway."

"Well," said Mother, sweeping up the nuts, "at least we've found a name for him. He's the craziest, nuttiest cat I have ever seen. We'll call him Filbert."

It wasn't quite daylight when Ronnie, awakened by another sound, heard the dogs whining eagerly. He tiptoed down and opened the front door. The little coon was rattling the door noisily.

Raffles had come home.

Maybe having the cat wasn't going to be so bad after all, he mused, as he crawled back into bed.

The next morning when Mother and Ronnie came into the kitchen Daddy was already there. He put his finger to his lips.

"Shush," he whispered. "Look, isn't this the cutest thing you have ever seen? Raffles and Filbert, curled up together, sleeping in the orphan box."

"Why didn't you want a cat, Daddy? I think they are awfully nice."

"Yes, they are nice, but not here in the wilds. Cats are predatory animals. No matter how well they are fed, they still hunt and kill. The squirrels, birds, and chipmunks will soon disappear with a cat around. You cannot blame a cat, because that is its nature, but I don't want it preying on all the small animals hereabouts."

"Oh, Filbert won't do that. We'll train him."

"You cannot train a cat not to hunt, Ronnie. It just isn't possible."

"Well," said Mother, "maybe we're just borrowing trouble. Let's see what happens. Maybe he won't do such a terrible thing."

But a few days later, Filbert proved that he really was a cat. He caught a chipmunk. Fortunately Ronnie was able to rescue it, but they all realized that the act would be repeated again and again until all the chipmunks and squirrels and birds were gone. It wasn't as if Filbert were hungry. He hunted just for fun.

Mother was the one who came up with a solution to the problem. She fastened a tiny bell to a collar and put it about Filbert's neck. He could now run and play as much as he liked, but he couldn't catch a thing, because the bell warned all the little creatures that Filbert was on the prowl and they would run and hide.

Filbert wasn't very happy about the bell, but everybody else was.

Daddy forgave Filbert for all of his shortcomings when a magazine editor bought the picture he had painted of Filbert and Raffles comfortably sleeping together.

Shortly thereafter, Filbert learned the danger that could lurk in the wilds for him.

One night they were all aroused by a terrible noise. Filbert had been left outside by mistake. The dogs were clamoring at the door, knowing that Filbert, who was now their friend and under their protection, was in grave danger.

Daddy grabbed a gun from his bedside table, and Mother grabbed another.

The cat's agonized sounds, mingled with other, louder sounds, came from a thicket a short distance from the house.

Daddy flashed his light into the thicket.

"It's a bobcat. A bobcat is death on house cats. I think he has killed Filbert."

The bobcat's eyes flashed yellow in the beam of light. Without a moment's hesitation, Mother raised her gun and fired at the yellow eyes.

The bobcat let out a terrible scream, and lay thrashing in the leaves for only a moment before it became still.

Mother rushed over to pick up the limp bloody bundle of fur that was Filbert.

"That was a wonderful shot, honey," Daddy said proudly. "I didn't know you knew how to use a gun."

"I don't. This is the first time I ever had one in my hands. I was just so mad about Filbert that I did it without thinking. Do you think I hurt the bobcat very much?"

"No, he hardly felt a thing. You killed him with one shot, right between the eyes."

"Lance! Lance! Filbert moved. He isn't dead. He is terribly chewed up and hurt, but he is still alive."

They carried Filbert into the kitchen and placed him gently in the orphan box, then bathed his wounds and covered him to keep him warm. There wasn't much more they could do for him tonight. They would just have to see if he was still alive in the morning.

The following morning Daddy gingerly opened the

orphan box, half afraid of what he might see.

Filbert opened one swollen eye, said a feeble *Meow,* and weakly swished his tail.

Daddy's eyes almost popped out of his head. "He's going to get well. I do believe cats have nine lives, though he nearly lost all nine of them. I expect he's hungry. Ronnie, get a can of salmon from the pantry."

Ronnie returned with a can of salmon. Daddy took one disdainful look at it.

"Oh, not that old pale salmon, Ronnie. That's cat salmon. Get him a can of the people's salmon, the best kind."

"It seems to me," said Ronnie, opening the salmon, "that this is mighty expensive salmon to be feeding a cat."

"It's just a temporary measure, Ronnie, but Filbert's had a very narrow escape and we must pamper his appetite."

It took two weeks for Filbert to recover fully, during which time he was so pampered that he became almost spoiled. And from then on he turned up his nose at cat salmon.

6

The ADOPTED GRANDMOTHER

ONE SATURDAY after chores were finished Ronnie started out to explore "the road." He had seen its beckoning curves every day from the school bus and imagined all sorts of strange and wonderful adventures awaiting him at its end. Surely the road led to some mysterious spot, and today was a splendid day to find out. Ralph had gone to Estes Park, and the dogs had disappeared on some strange mission of their own, so Ronnie started out alone, taking his emergency whistle in case he got lost.

Bluejays and magpies flitted in and out among the evergreens, and now and then a bustling squirrel jumping from limb to limb shook pine needles down on him. He saw a big hawk swoop down, and rise again with a small object in its cruel talons. Only a few days before, Daddy had found a dead hawk and had shown Ronnie what a very wide wingspread it had. They did not look very large when flying far overhead, but they were among the most powerful and predatory of birds, hunting smaller birds, rabbits, squirrels, and chipmunks; yet they were necessary too, for they kept field mice and other rodents from overrunning the land. There were other birds of prey constantly flitting through the forests of Colorado — the gorgeous magpie, probably the most beautiful of all birds, and the mighty eagle, who came from the high crags in the distance.

Ronnie walked up the luring, beckoning little road. Except that it was cut through a steep canyon which rose on either side, and there were no signs of travel, it seemed, after all, little different from other trails.

A big porcupine lumbered into the bushes. Ronnie was surprised to see that they grew so large — almost as big as a bear cub, and a good-sized bear cub at that.

He had heard about the time Penny had attacked a porcupine she had come upon eating the handle off a hoe. Porcupines like the taste of the salty human perspiration left on tools people have handled and touched. That was before Penny had learned the meaning of the word "stop." She got a noseful of quills, which had to be removed with tweezers and treated with a mixture of castor oil and Lysol to keep the sore spots from becoming infected. Penny never got close to a porcupine after this. And from then on she too knew what the word "stop" meant.

Ronnie had walked for some time when he smelled wood smoke. Rounding a curve, he saw a tiny cabin with smoke rising from its chimney. He was walking past it when the door opened and a little old lady called to him.

"Hello, there!" she said. "You weren't going to walk right on past, were you? Visitors don't come up this way very often. Please come in."

In the living room there was a fire blazing in a fireplace made of strange silvery stones. Ronnie knew the stones were mica. He had recently found one for his collection.

It was a pretty, crowded little room, full of old-fashioned pictures of people in strange, outdated clothing. There were plants on the window ledges, and two big cats lay before the fire. In a large cage near a sunny window was a one-legged bluebird.

"You must be Lance O'Leary's boy." The little old lady smiled. "I don't believe I've seen you before. My name is Mrs. Tayton, and I live here all alone, so you will have to come and visit me often, now that you have found the way."

At Mrs. Tayton's invitation, Ronnie removed his coat and hung it on a peg.

"I always hope someone may come to visit, so I try

to have something on hand to serve. I made dough-nuts today. Do you like doughnuts and cookies?" the little old lady asked.

She reached for the biggest cookie jar Ronnie had ever seen. It was bright and blue, and full of cookies and doughnuts.

They drank milk and Ronnie ate doughnuts until he lost count. Mrs. Tayton ate hers more slowly and told him about the two old cats and about the bluebird in the cage.

"I found him in the woods about two years ago. One of his legs was gone and one wing broken. He may have been attacked by a hawk. I couldn't leave the poor little thing to die, so I brought him home to care for until he was well. He recovered but of course could not grow a new leg, and his wing never healed properly. He looked so miserable — fluttering along the ground, unable to hop or fly — that I have kept him in this cage ever since. He watches the birds come and go outside the window and sometimes joins in their songs. He has been company for me. I guess we needed each other."

She was the loveliest little old lady Ronnie had ever seen, something like a bird herself, quick and spry and cheerful. Her round eyes were even bluer than Mother's. Curling white hair was knotted neatly on top of

her head, and her complexion was the smoothest peach-and-white Ronnie had ever seen.

Mrs. Tayton asked him so many questions that Ronnie knew she had not talked with anyone for a long time and was very lonely. She soon knew all about Ronnie and his family. She already knew Daddy, but she had to hear about Mother, and the animal members of the family as well.

"Now, tell me about your family," Ronnie said, knowing it was rude to monopolize the conversation. "Don't you have a family?"

"Oh, yes. But they have all been dead for a very long time. The sad thing about growing old is that very often an old person finds herself alone, the only one remaining of her friends and family. That is very lonely."

"Do you mean that of all the friends you ever had, not one is left?" asked Ronnie, thinking how desolate that would be.

"Almost," she said. "Of course, there is still old Tom Blake, who came here to prospect for gold and silver many years ago and never left. He still prospects in these mountains, although he is past eighty years old."

She gave the bluebird a doughnut crumb.

"But why didn't you go to the city where people could look out for you?"

"Oh, this is my home. I wouldn't want to live anyplace else. Even though the road is snowbound in winter, folks do drop in now and then. Your daddy comes to visit me, and to see if I need anything from town. Then when Tom Blake comes back in the spring, we have a very gay time, playing checkers and talking about the old days during the gold and silver rush when all our friends were living."

That didn't sound very gay to Ronnie. It sounded lonely and sad.

"Don't you even have any grandchildren?"

"No," said Mrs. Tayton, looking almost as if she were going to cry. "But I would love to have a grandchild more than anything else in the world, a grandchild who would come to visit sometimes. I could keep the cookie jar filled and he and I could talk about all kinds of things."

Ronnie looked about the cozy little room, and at the firelight shining on Mrs. Tayton's white hair. In all his life he had never had a grandmother. He had often thought about how nice it would be to have a "cookie jar" grandmother to visit, like some of the other boys he had known. He patted her hand.

"If you don't mind," Ronnie said hopefully, "I'd like to use you for my grandmother."

Mrs. Tayton's tinkling laughter filled the tiny room.

"It's been a very long time since anyone has used me for anything. I can't think of a nicer fate, or anyone whose grandmother I would rather be. And, of course, if you are to be my grandson, I'll have to adopt the rest of the family too. Do you think your parents will mind?"

"Of course not. They don't care what I bring home."

"Well," she laughed, "you won't be taking me home with you. I'll just remain here in my own little house, handy for you to come to visit. That is nicer, don't you think?"

"Well, if you ever want to move in with us, you just come. We have lots of room. But I think I had better go now. Mother will be worrying."

Grandmother Tayton put four plump sugary dough-nuts in a sack and handed them to him.

"Four for the road," she twinkled.

Opening the door, she put her arms around him and kissed him, just as if she had always been his grand-mother.

The bluebird fluttered its broken wing happily.

Ronnie fairly leaped along the road. Just as he had

known it would, the road had had a wonderful adventure at its end.

Last year he and Mother and Bugs and Mitzi had been all alone. And suddenly they had acquired a large, assorted family. And today he had adopted a grandmother, just as he had adopted a daddy, choosing them out of the whole world.

There was no place on earth so magical as Tattercoat Range.

7

DRIFTER, *the Horse,*

and LADDIE, *the Dog*

Few things in Ronnie's new life were as exciting as going on field trips with Daddy. Sometimes Daddy painted, drew, or took photographs of the many wonders of the forest. Other times they merely walked, or camped, while Daddy told Ronnie fascinating stories of the wild animals living in the high mountains of Tattercoat Range. Once in a while they went with Mr. Mallow to still higher places, where the bighorn sheep leaped from crag to crag in a world of ice and snow. It was one of Mr. Mallow's duties to estimate the number of each species of animal on the game preserve. The Forestry Department took this game poll to determine the amount of food necessary to feed the animals.

Once Ronnie went with Daddy to a deserted little town, many miles above the small gray house on Tattercoat Range. During the gold-and-silver-rush days it had been a busy town full of people. Long

since abandoned and fallen to ruin, it was now called
Forsaken Village. The trail was rough and faint. And
there, much to Ronnie's surprise were the unmistakable tracks of Ole Cripple Toe. Only a few nights before, he had heard the big wolf and his smaller mate
howling quite close to Tattercoat Range.

On the way home from Forsaken Village, Daddy
pointed to an animal scurrying over the pine needles
and through the berry bushes. It was a fox.

"Why, he's black-and-white!" whispered Ronnie. "I
thought wild foxes were red or gray. All the others I've
seen around here are."

"Yes, most of them are," said Daddy softly so as not
to frighten the fox. "The little fellow you have just
seen was not always a wild fox. At least his ancestors
weren't. There are many fur ranches in Colorado, but
fortunately for the foxes the demand for silver-fox furs
has gradually lessened. One rancher who had a fox
farm not far from here could no longer afford to feed
the animals. Rather than kill them, he let them go
free. Some of them wandered onto Tattercoat Range,
where they mated and raised their young. I think
there are about thirty of them here now, not counting
the spring litters."

"Aren't they beautiful?" said Ronnie, watching the
full brush of the fox's tail disappear over the ridge.

"They are among the most beautiful of all fur-bearing animals, and certainly one of the most intelligent and crafty. A fox and his mate, the vixen, can torment dogs for hours, completely bewildering them. When the dogs chase them, the foxes double back, crossing and recrossing each other's trail. They take each other's place in the chase, one resting while the other comes in with new energy. The foxes remain fresh but the dogs become exhausted, thinking it is one fox they are chasing when it is really two. Usually the foxes escape and wind up watching the dogs from some concealed place."

"That's being smart," Ronnie agreed.

"Living in the wilds as they do, foxes have no human help and they have to be intelligent. Take getting rid of fleas, for example. The crafty fox swims out into a pond or stream with a stick in his mouth. He immerses himself except for his nose and the stick, which remain above the water. The fleas crawl onto the stick to escape the water, and then the fox straightway drops it and swims out, minus the fleas."

Nearing home they came to a pool lying still and deep. A fallen tree that had been broken in a storm lay across it, forming a bridge. Down from the mountains and below the silent pool rushed a crystal stream on its way to join the big rivers which part at the Continental

Divide. The Continental Divide, Daddy explained, is an imaginary trail where all of the waters of the land separate, some going one way to join the mighty Pacific Ocean, others plunging toward the Atlantic. By following this trail a man can walk from the Canadian border to the border of Mexico without once crossing a stream, or even getting his feet wet. That was something Ronnie had not known.

"That pool is the haunt of Old-Timer, a friendly foe of mine," Daddy continued most reverently, as if Old-Timer were very special.

"How can anything be a friend and a foe at the same time?" Ronnie asked.

Daddy stood looking at the pool. "Old-Timer is a huge trout, the granddaddy of them all. He has lived here for many years, swimming back and forth across the pool and up and down the stream. But the pool is really his home. Every year I try to catch and land him, but always fail. I have hooked him, but never landed him. The best fishermen in Colorado have tried for him too. Some have hooked him, but he has always gotten away. There are several hooks in his tough mouth now, but he still swims freely and gallantly. To me he is much more than a trout. He is a valiant foe, waging his life against my skill, and one respects so courageous an adversary, as greatly as one respects a friend. This year I suppose I will try for him again, and as usual he will let me hook him and think I have almost landed him, then he'll break the line and swim away laughing — that is, if trout laugh.

"To tell you the truth, I hope no one ever lands him. I like to think of his remaining here unconquered. I hope he never meets the fisherman who is smarter than he is, but if anyone ever does land him, I am going to shake that fellow's hand and pin a medal on him, for he will be one of the best fishermen of all time."

A black mother bear and her two cubs were tearing at the berry bushes across the stream. Daddy snapped some pictures of the plump cubs tumbling and playing like fat little boys in a game of hide-and-seek. One of the cubs decided to come down the hillside, but instead of walking or running down, he made himself into a round, furry ball, and rolled.

"Do you know why bear cubs roll down a slope?" Daddy asked.

"To get down, I guess, or just for fun. Bears have the most fun of anyone."

"That is true, but it is also true that bears have no breastbone, and their forelegs are very close together. This makes it difficult for them to balance when coming down a slope, so it is easier for them to roll down."

They crossed the stream at the otters' village, noticing the otters' muddy slides slipping down into the water.

It was on a field trip during Easter vacation that Ronnie and Daddy found the horse. They were in the mountains miles from home, where although much of the snow had melted some of it still lay in deep drifts. It would never melt completely because of the shortness of the summer.

Sitting on a log, nibbling their sandwiches, they noticed something dark in the middle of one of the distant drifts.

"I wonder what it is?" Daddy mused. "Probably a deer stuck in the deep snow."

But it wasn't a deer. It was a horse, so deep in the snow that he couldn't get out. Getting as close to the animal as possible, Daddy took the rope he always carried on trips and made a lasso. After several tries, he finally encircled the horse's neck. He wound the other end of the rope around a tree to keep it from slipping out of their hands and to give them something strong to pull against. They pulled as hard as they could, a steady pull, because any sudden jerk might break the horse's neck. As it was, they were afraid they might strangle the horse. Daddy had freed deer from drifts many times, but that was much easier, for the animal wasn't as heavy and the buck could be lassoed around the horns.

Finally they could feel the other end of the rope loosen and give a bit. Still they pulled, perspiration running down their faces in spite of the coolness of the air. At last the horse came free. But such a horse! He was merely skin and bones.

"There's no knowing how long he has been in that drift," Daddy said. "The snow has furnished him water, but he has been without food. I don't know why he hasn't frozen, probably because he was protected from the wind by the blanket of snow. It's a good thing he was able to keep his head above the snow."

The horse seemed to be no color at all, just dark with the dampness of the snow. Starvation had played havoc with his coat and flesh, and his eyes were dull and tired-looking. They led him to some tender grass where the snow had melted. He could hardly stand. The lumps of sugar which they always carried were the only other food they had for him.

Daddy stood looking sorrowfully at the skin and bones, which only by a stretch of the imagination resembled a horse.

"Son," he said slowly, "walk on ahead, over the hill."

"What are you going to do?"

"I have to shoot him, Ronnie, that's the merciful thing to do. He is almost dead already."

Ronnie gulped, but didn't argue. Daddy didn't like to shoot anything. In all the time Ronnie had known him, Daddy always carried a gun into the forest, but Ronnie had never seen him use it. And now, if he said he had to shoot the poor horse, he just had to shoot it, that's all, but he didn't want Ronnie to have to watch the execution.

Ronnie walked sorrowfully over the brow of the slope and waited. He waited for quite a while, but heard no gunshot. Then he saw why. Daddy was coming, supporting the horse in such a way that he seemed to be carrying it.

"You couldn't do it, could you?" Ronnie smiled.

Daddy shook his head. "No, not after all the poor fellow has been through. But we can't leave him here. He would die of exposure from the cold wind, or the wolves would get him. Maybe he was running from them when he fell into the snowdrift. We'll just have to try to get him home."

They unfolded their camp blankets, which they

carried in rolls across their shoulders, and placed them over the horse's back. It would take them hours to reach home, for the horse could hardly stand, much less walk. Very slowly, letting him rest every few minutes, they started down the mountain.

It was painful to watch the horse make the gallant effort to hobble along. His bones almost protruded through his pathetic coat. He leaned against Daddy part of the way. Every minute Ronnie expected him to give up the effort and lie down and die.

It had been late in the day when they rescued the horse, and hours had passed since then. Their flashlights blinked through the darkness, reflecting the shining eyes of the animals who came out at night. Now and then they could hear soft padding steps behind them, and knew that they were being followed and watched by a mountain lion, or by Ole Cripple Toe and his mate.

Daddy looked at his watch. "It's two o'clock, almost daylight. Mother will be wild with worry. Eat a chocolate bar, Ronnie, to build up your energy."

Ronnie dug a chocolate bar from his pocket, and another for Daddy. Such food was a necessity in the mountains.

Suddenly they heard a shot, an alien sound in these mountains. Daddy answered with three rapid shots in the air, the woodsman's signal for help. The poor horse jumped a little at the sound of the shots, and trembled, which was all he could manage with the little strength he had left.

Soon they saw two lights bobbing through the darkness ahead, and Daddy shouted. Mr. Mallow and Mr. Glenn, another forest ranger, answered.

When the two rangers reached them, everyone expressed his relief and happiness, and the hot coffee which Mr. Mallow had tasted wonderful.

"That was the longest eight miles I ever covered," Daddy said, refilling his cup from the thermos. "We've been on the way since yesterday afternoon."

"I told Laurie that if we found you and everything was all right, I'd fire two shots," said Mr. Mallow, promptly firing into the sky. "She was terribly worried, thought maybe you had broken a leg or something, so she phoned us for help."

With everyone bracing the horse, the rest of the journey was easier.

"I don't know how he ever made it," said Mr. Mallow, lifting the blankets and viewing the horse's ribs. "It's only that he is a young horse and was very strong to start with."

Mother certainly was happy to see them, and almost

cried about the poor horse. She thought he would
die in a few hours, not believing anything that thin
could live. But she wasn't angry that they had caused
her to worry — she just smiled very gently.

Daddy rushed out to the barn and cleared a square
place for the animal, then stacked bales of hay high,
to make it warm. They hunted out all the camp
blankets to cover the horse, and fed him warm mash, a
little at a time, as starving creatures have to be fed
after a long fast. A bucket of water was put by him,
and then the little shelter was closed with more bales
of hay.

After they had eaten the ham and eggs, hot coffee,
and chocolate milk Mother had waiting for them in
the warm kitchen, Ronnie went up to bed. Lying
there, wide awake, he listened to the voices coming up
from the kitchen below.

"Now where is Mitzi?" Mother asked.

"Oh, naturally she is in the barn with the sick horse,
trying to mother him," Daddy answered. "She thinks
she's needed there."

"Well, Lance," said Mr. Mallow, "I hope your good
deed was not in vain, but the way that horse looks to
me, I don't know. And there's no telling where he
came from. He has no brand. Maybe he escaped from

a ranch, or maybe he's one of the wild fellows, lost from the herd. You can't tell."

Daddy said, "If we ever find his owner, I'd like to buy him, or at least let him know what happened to the horse."

Ronnie called down the staircase, "Well, since he's a drifter from 'most anyplace, and we found him in a snowdrift — I'd like to name him Drifter."

"An excellent name," said Mr. Mallow. "But you must prepare yourself, Ronnie, he may not live, you know."

But Ronnie knew the horse would live. Because they wanted him to, and were pulling for him so hard. And because of the magic of Tattercoat Range.

When they went out to see him at daylight, the horse was lying down in the snug little house of hay, with Mitzi cuddled against his head. And he was alive! They fed him again, and Daddy brushed his shabby coat.

"He's a sorrel, with a platinum mane and tail. If he pulls through, he'll be a beauty. He's about three years old, and has never been shod, which probably means he belongs to no one, particularly since he has never been branded, either."

"He belongs to us!" said Ronnie. "And I don't care

whether he's a beauty or not. I just want him to live."

"If it's humanly possible, son, we'll save him," said Daddy, patting Ronnie's worried head.

Mr. Mallow came by and gave the horse a big shot of penicillin to keep him from getting pneumonia. All their friends dropped by to see him, except Grandmother Tayton, who couldn't come that distance, so Ronnie went to tell her about Drifter.

Grandmother Tayton listened very quietly, then said, "I'm sure he will get well with you and your father to give him such good care. Lance O'Leary would have made a wonderful doctor. There is a saddle here which my husband always used, and I would like you to have it. He always rode a sorrel horse, too."

The saddle had been oiled and packed away for many years, but its dark leather gleamed and the silver trim shone brightly from many rubbings. It was the most beautiful saddle Ronnie had ever seen, though he thought how strange this saddle would look on poor Drifter.

That night they heard a dog bark, but since this was not unusual, no one paid any attention. The next morning they found a strange dog lying on the ground beside Timothy Tattercoat. He was a springer spaniel, dark brown and white, with long, fluffy ears and a short tail.

Daddy called, "You lost, fellow? Come here, boy. Come on, lad."

The dog rose to his feet and almost fell as he stumbled toward the outstretched hand. His stubby tail wagged feebly.

"He likes us, Daddy." cried Ronnie. "He's wagging his tail."

But Daddy looked worried. "Are you blind, lad?" He took the dog's head between his gentle hands and looked into his eyes. "No, you're not blind. I guess you're sick."

"I wonder who he belongs to?" Ronnie asked.

"Well, there are no dogs like this for miles around. I know them all. He may have been lost from some tourist's car. We will try to find the owner. Whoever he is, he must feel badly about losing such a fine and valuable dog."

The animal lay there wagging his stubby tail feebly as Daddy patted him and worked his fingers through his long hair.

"This dog," he said huskily, "is starving to death! He has been badly beaten."

The dog, like poor Drifter, was merely skin and

bones. They hadn't noticed this, or the purple whip marks before, because his body was so well covered by long, tangled hair.

"Get a blanket, son."

"There aren't any camp blankets left. They are all on Drifter."

"Well, get one of Mother's good ones, then."

They wrapped the blanket around the dog, carried him inside, and made a bed for him in the kitchen beside the Iron Maiden. He was much too big to go into the orphan box.

Mother heated some milk and fed it to him gently, for his mouth was sore from starvation. He looked up at her gratefully.

"Imagine anyone in the world treating a dog as this one has been treated!" Daddy said angrily.

The other dogs seemed to know that the spaniel was sick. They didn't bark or growl. Mitzi was in a quandary. She couldn't decide which needed her more, the sick horse or the sick dog. She must have lost half a pound chasing from one sick creature to the other, worried and perplexed.

No one ever really named the dog. Daddy had called him "poor lad," so Lad, or Laddie, he became. They ran ads in the Denver papers, put a notice up in the general store on the highway, and asked everyone they met, but no one ever claimed him. Both he and Drifter remained mysteries as long as they lived.

In three days Laddie was well enough to be bathed and have his coat brushed. He began to regain his weight, and his coat grew silkier every day.

Drifter mended more slowly, still in his house of hay, although every day he did grow a little stronger. His coat became a little more glossy, his eyes a little brighter, and he ate more with each meal. Then one day, he nosed the bales of hay away from the door and trotted out into the open.

With the blankets off and the sunshine splashing on him, he was resplendent in his satin-like coat, which had been so carefully tended. It was a dark lustrous sorrel, and his flowing mane and tail were silver-white. He carried his head with an arrogant grace, like a fine-blooded animal. Hesitantly he approached the O'Learys, gently blowing in their hair, and presently nosing into their pockets for apples and the lump sugar which Ronnie had come to call "horse candy."

A few days later Ronnie and Daddy took him to the blacksmith shop at the lumber mill to have his hoofs trimmed and shod. They talked of riding him when he grew stronger.

Several weeks later when Ronnie got off the school bus an amazing sight met his eyes — Daddy, dressed in Western riding garb, was on Drifter's back. Drifter trotted with arched neck, silver mane and tail waving in the breeze. Mr. Tayton's ornate old saddle shone with polishing, and the silver shimmered in the sunlight. It didn't look strange on Drifter at all. It was exactly right. The dogs ran and scampered about, happily chasing and barking at the sight, and even Filbert, who by this time thought he was a dog too, ran along beside them.

Daddy lifted Ronnie into the saddle, and together they rode home.

On their next camping trip Ronnie thought they might have solved the mystery of Drifter's origin — but he could never be sure. He and Daddy had gone to the high Sangre de Cristo Mountains. The mountains, on the border of Colorado and New Mexico, are wild and rugged, with some sections still unexplored.

One evening at twilight they climbed up on a high precipice to look at an eagle's nest. Lance told him about how the eagles mated for life, and how the parent birds together shared the care of their young, that it was against the law to shoot or cage these wild, free creatures. Ronnie could not imagine anyone wanting to. It would be like trying to cage the wind.

Looking down from the high ledge into the deep

mountain canyon where the white rising moon had spread a silvery-green tone, Daddy exclaimed, "Look! There is a wild-horse herd, probably descendants of the horses lost here by the Spanish conquistadors of Coronado over four hundred years ago. Before they came there were no horses on the North American Continent."

The lovely, wild creatures ran like the wind, racing through the moonlit valley, happy and free.

"Sometimes horses escape from the ranches and join the wild herd," Daddy continued. "They are led by a giant palomino stallion, and always have been. Each leader has looked so much alike that no one knows when the younger one takes over, and some persist in saying that it is the same stallion who never grows old, and who never dies. But that, of course, is only a legend. Many men have tried, over the years, to capture the leader — he is such a beautiful, crafty, powerful animal. Fortunately, no one has ever succeeded."

"It's a big herd, isn't it? Is it bigger than the herd you told me sometimes runs in our mountains?"

"Well, son, you know state lines do not mean anything to horses. They cross over the mountains between Colorado and New Mexico, and range for miles and miles, moving on to greener pastures over both states," Daddy explained, lighting his pipe. "It is the very same herd. Those mountains which you see dimly in the distance surround Tattercoat Range.

"This is the herd I've always felt our Drifter came from. He may even be one of the sons of the great leader. Perhaps he would have been the next to lead them over the mountains and down into the valleys on feet like the wings of the wind. Who knows?"

8

ROSY GLOW, *the Personality Pig*

Rᴏɴɴɪᴇ ᴡᴀᴠᴇᴅ as he rode past Elsa Pittman's house on Drifter.

"Oh, Ronnie, come here! I want to show you something."

He tied Drifter to the fence and went to see what Elsa had. It was a litter of tiny pigs. They were the first he had ever seen. Elsa said it would disturb the mother pig if they went too close, so they peered through the bars of the pen. One tiny pig stood alone, shaking and shivering.

"That's the runt," Elsa said sadly. "The others won't let it eat, so my father is going to have to kill it. None of us has time to raise it on a bottle, we have so many other chores."

The little pig continued to shiver. The mother pig didn't want it because it wasn't as fat and healthy as the others she was busy feeding and protecting. Ronnie reached through the bars and pulled the thin little pig

to him. It sucked his ear as if trying to get milk. Ronnie laughed. He was delighted.

"May I take it home?" he asked. "We have lots of time to feed him on a bottle."

"Sure," Elsa said happily. "I knew you'd take him."

She gave him one of her baby brother's bottles and rubber nipples. Those on Tattercoat Range were beginning to wear out from feeding so many helpless animals.

They put the little pig in an empty flour sack, and tied him securely to Drifter's saddle horn. He squealed all the way home.

Mother and Daddy were outside someplace, probably watching the baby otters slide down the slippery slide. Ronnie took the little pig into the kitchen and put it in the orphan box, now abandoned by Raffles. Filbert, the only one at home, came to investigate the new arrival. Since the little pig was still shivering, Ronnie covered it with straw. Now nothing could be seen of it and the only sign of its presence was the moving straw caused by its breathing. This fascinated Filbert, who hopped into the box and slapped gently at the straw before cuddling down with the tiny pig.

Ronnie had the fire going when Mother and Daddy came home. This always pleased Mother very much.

She removed her jacket and put shortening in the pan for frying chicken.

Ronnie wondered how best to break the news of the little pig to Mother.

Finally he said, "Mother, you'll never guess what I have brought you. It's the nicest surprise; something I think you've never had before. Guess what it is."

Mother smiled happily. Sometimes, depending on what it was, she loved surprises.

"Columbines?" she guessed.

"Aw, you've had them before. It's something you'll really like."

"Wild iris?" Mother guessed, flouring the chicken.

"No," Ronnie said, nervously watching the moving straw.

Mother finally gave up.

"It's in the orphan box," Ronnie said.

"Oh, I might have known!" Mother cried. "Ronnie, I've just finished raising a bunch of little wood mice. Daddy took them out today and put them in a thicket in an abandoned goldfinch nest. And I don't want anything else."

"Well, you'll want this," said Ronnie, uncovering the little white pig.

"What in the world —" gasped Mother. "It looks

like — Oh, no, Ronald. It isn't a pig?"

When Mother said "Ronald" she meant business. The little pig had almost stopped shivering when Ronnie lifted it out of the box.

"You'll have to take it back, Ronald. Where in the world would we keep a pig?"

"But the Pittmans will have to kill it because it can't eat by itself. Maybe if I keep him a few days he can learn to eat out of a pan, and get fat. Then I can take him back."

"All right," Mother replied, putting the chicken in the pan. "But it's your responsibility. I can't be bothered with it, with all I have to do. Here, I'll fill the bottle for you."

She heated the milk, filled the bottle, and tested it on her arm.

Smack, smack, smack, went the little hungry animal, and in no time at all the bottle was empty.

"People must think we really are a Trailside Museum — always dumping their animals off on us," Mother stormed.

"Well, what else can they think?" asked Daddy, rubbing the little pig.

"That pig has to go to the barn or woodshed," scolded Mother. "Who ever heard of a pig in the house?"

Daddy just raised his eyebrows and kept on scratching. The little pig looked blissfully happy.

"Okay," agreed Ronnie, feeling sorry for Mother, who always had so much work to do. But he felt sorrier for the little pig. "As soon as it gets good and warm, I'll take it out to the old cold barn."

The dogs were scratching at the door to come in. They looked with mild interest at the pig. They were so used to new arrivals being in the orphan box they didn't seem a bit surprised. Mitzi, of course, was utterly delighted.

After Mother and Daddy and Ronnie had eaten the chicken, which for some strange reason had been burned in places, Mother picked up the tiny animal. It grabbed her ear and started sucking on it.

She laughed merrily, just as Ronnie had done. "This is the cutest little animal I've ever seen. But a pig! They grow to be enormous."

"Laurie," said Daddy, "do you remember the one you had when you were a little girl, that finally grew so big your father had to buy a farm to keep it on?"

Mother frowned and shook her head. "Lance, you hush."

Ronnie pretended he hadn't heard, and said, "I kind of thought I'd like to be a Future Farmer of America and maybe start with this little pig."

Daddy thought this was a good idea — animals could work for them for a change. "With this little pig, and the vegetable garden which you and Mother and Mr. Paulsen are planting tomorrow, you will be right in business."

"The only reason we have to hire Mr. Paulsen to help around the place is because we have so many animals," Mother retorted.

"Then one more can't matter," Daddy pointed out.

"Look!" Mother shrieked, almost dropping the little pig, to Mitzi's great concern. "This pig has lice, hog lice!"

"What did you expect — butterflies?" Daddy asked.

"Well, that settles it. We're not having any pest-infected animals around this place."

"How did you get the lice off the little pig you used to have? Remember?" Daddy asked.

Mother ignored him.

She dumped soap powder in the old washtub which was used for bathing animals and filled it with warm water tested with her elbow.

EEEEEEEEEK! squealed the little pig the minute it hit the water, its tiny black hoofs tattooing the sides of the tub.

"This is a little girl pig, Ronnie, so you will have to stop calling her 'him,' " Mother said, scrubbing the pig briskly with an old vegetable brush. It didn't take long to bathe a pig only about eight inches long.

She dried her gently. "Look how white she is, and her skin is as pink as a baby's. She positively has a rosy glow."

"That's a good name," cried Ronnie, wondering whether a pig's tail curled to the left or to the right. "Rosy Glow! She's my start toward becoming a Future Farmer of America."

Mother poured pink-clover cologne on Rosy Glow, saying that it seemed an appropriate fragrance for a pig.

"Well," mused Daddy, "she may not be the biggest or the finest pig in the world, but she is certainly the sweetest-smelling one, I'll wager."

Mother refilled the milk bottle, and the little pig gulped hungrily.

"Now, Ronald, remember," Mother said firmly, "I'm simply not going to start taking care of this pig. It's your job, so don't you forget it for an instant. And remember, pigs never seem to get enough to eat."

Daddy laughed until the tears rolled down his face, but Mother couldn't see what was so funny.

"Will she grow up to be a big sow and have pigs?" asked Ronnie, busy with his plans of being a Future Farmer of America.

"Ronald!" cried Mother. "Don't use that terrible word. Don't you dare call this cute little thing a sow. This pig is as clean as a puppy," she defended.

"Of course it is," Daddy answered. "Pigs are not naturally dirty animals. They like to be clean, but when they are kept in dirty pens and fed garbage and slop they cannot help getting dirty and smelly."

"Well, Rosy Glow is always going to have a clean pen. I'll see to that," Ronnie stated.

"I expect that baby pigs can eat cereal if it is cooked as carefully as babies' food," Mother added.

"Yes, but who will have time to do that?" Ronnie asked.

"Well, since you will be in school and Daddy is busy making a living, I guess I will."

Rosy Glow soon learned that it was Mother who usually fed her, and when she heard Mother's heels *tap-tap* across the floor, she would stand on her hind legs, with her front hoofs no bigger than a minute on the edge of the box, and squeal and squeal.

Mother laughed. "That pig practically calls me Mother."

Stuffed with milk and carefully prepared oatmeal several times a day, Rosy Glow grew so fat that she had to be moved into the woodshed. She stayed nice and clean, however, and thanks to Mother, no lice appeared on her again. Ronnie put clean straw in her box every day.

Filbert spent a great deal of time on the edge of the box, watching the little pig. Daddy thought this was such an unusual friendship he painted a picture of them together. There certainly was no accounting, Mother mused, for some of the strange attachments among animals. The cat rebelled only when Rosy Glow lay down on him. Pigs, no matter how small they are, are heavy animals.

Rosy didn't stay in her box for long. She soon discovered a pile of coal that she liked to eat, or root into, or scatter all over the woodshed. There was no box strong enough to keep her in. And then came the day when she got into the tender little vegetables in the garden. Mother almost cried. But that was not as bad as the day they all returned from town to find that Rosy had opened the bag of choice tulip bulbs for which Mother had saved all winter — and eaten every one of them.

"I wonder," Daddy said, "how bacon tastes if raised on tulip bulbs?"

"Well, I don't know; but I for one would welcome the chance to find out," Mother stormed.

But she didn't mean it. She couldn't really eat a bite of Rosy Glow.

The little pig eventually rebelled at being a lone pig, and ran squealing after the dogs whenever she got a chance.

"All the animals around this place think they are dogs," Ronnie said, watching the play.

"All except the dogs, and they think they are people," Mother retorted.

The dogs were surprisingly gentle, although occasionally when the play got rough, the little pig was sent squealing to the sanctity of the woodshed to be soothed by Mother and Mitzi. Once, however, when a neighboring rancher's dog came into the yard, all the O'Leary dogs ran to Rosy's aid when the dog came too close, and they chased him from the yard.

Rosy Glow soon had to be moved from the woodshed to the barn, where she was put in the strongest pen Daddy and Mr. Paulsen could make. It was never quite strong enough, however. Rosy could always get out, usually in search of a mud puddle or a wallow, and it didn't matter to her where she made that wallow either. She would overturn the lawn furniture, knock the washtub from the outside wall of the house, and always find her way back to the garden.

No doubt about it, Rosy Glow was a pest. But then there was the fair — the big county fair.

Rosy Glow was once more washed and polished. Her pink ears were cleaned and her black hoofs shined. Every inch of her fat two hundred pounds was so white and rosy that Mother couldn't resist spraying her again with cologne.

Rosy walked up the plank of Ralph's father's truck with hardly any coaxing at all. All Ronnie had to do was hold some carrots under her nose and she followed him into the truck. But then Rosy never had been able to resist cars. One time a friend from Denver had left his car in the yard with the door open. Much to Rosy's delight and Mother's embarrassment, the pig had wedged herself firmly into the front seat, so firmly that it seemed to Daddy he would have to use a blow torch to remove her. But that hadn't been necessary after all. All they had to do was remove the steering wheel and Rosy climbed out by herself.

When they reached the fairgrounds, Rosy was put in her pen in the livestock building and left there with the other animals until the day of judging. Every time her family left her during the next three days Rosy Glow put her shiny, manicured hoofs on the gate and squealed and squealed.

On the last day the judges came and examined the animals. Rosy Glow welcomed them with squeals of joy, her white bristles shining, her skin glowing, and her tail curling like a corkscrew. She was so glad to see them, being tired of having nothing but animals around. The men looked at her, at her registration papers, and left.

An hour later, after having examined all the other pigs, they came back and fastened a blue ribbon on Rosy's stall. In gold letters it read, FIRST PRIZE; and the judges gave Ronnie a money prize in addition. He was so happy that he hugged Rosy's big, fat neck, which still smelled of pink clover. In fact, one of the judges said, "You know, this pig really has a sweet disposition. She doesn't smell the way pigs usually do. She smells something like clover or sweet grass. You would think she had been raised like a human baby."

"Well, she was," Ronnie said, full of pride and happiness. "Rosy and I practically have the same mother."

Ronnie wanted to divide the money with Mother because, after all, she had certainly helped raise his pig, and there was the matter of the tulip bulbs. But she smilingly refused his offer.

On the way home he was busy making plans for next year's fair. He was made now. He was a genuine, full-fledged Future Farmer of America. He would enter Rosy Glow again, of course, and some of the chickens, and maybe get a milk goat or two. There was going to be lots of responsibility and work connected with being a Future Farmer of America, he knew, and probably a *little* assistance from Mother.

For many days afterward, Rosy Glow basked in the sunshine of her success, loving the attention and scratching and praise heaped upon her.

Daddy said, "Well, she deserves a mud puddle like other plain, ordinary pigs, and, by jiminy, she's going to have it."

And she did.

The next year Rosy Glow and her litter did take an even bigger prize. She repaid her family well for having bottle-raised and tulip-bulb-fed her. Every year she had more pigs, until there were pigs all over the place. Unfortunately, they all inherited their mother's destructive habits, but they too were valued and privileged animals.

9

LODGE, *the Elk*

HIGH ABOVE the little gray house on Tattercoat Range, a large elk herd ranged. Sometimes they came down into the lowlands and even crossed the road. That's why signs were scattered along the highway reading GAME CROSSING, DRIVE CAREFULLY, and DEER CROSSING.

They were beautiful creatures with spreading antlers, and graceful heads and necks. They were really a species of giant deer, that when fully grown outweighed a pony. Like the other wild creatures in the game preserve, the wild elk on Tattercoat Range had never been hunted. They seemed instinctively to know the boundary lines, seldom wandering down to the areas where during the hunting season men waited with guns.

They fed on the lush grass, and bushes, and on the tender leaves of the "quaking" aspen, that small silver-white tree whose leaves turn golden in the fall, and is called "quaking" because the leaves are never still, moving with each small breeze and even when there is no breeze at all.

Ronnie had often watched the herd through binoculars, and had thought the elk the most regal, the most beautiful of all the wild creatures. He liked to hear their hoofs thundering over the stones and across the mountain meadows in the distance. Daddy had told him that there could be as many as fifteen-hundred elk in a single herd.

And then one day they had an elk of their very own. Legally, too, because Mr. Mallow, the forest ranger, brought it to them and helped them put it in the big barn, which was empty now except for Drifter, Rosy Glow, Trader Horn, and Nan, the new burro Daddy had bought to use on pack trips instead of a jeep (much to Ronnie's delight, because one couldn't pat a jeep).

Mr. Mallow had driven up the lane and stopped near the barn, calling for Daddy, Mr. Paulsen, and Ronnie to help him unload the elk.

"Lance, I'd appreciate it if you would allow me to keep this young elk calf in your barn for a time. Our stalls at the ranger station are all full, and I know you have lots of room here."

"Where did you get an elk?" Ronnie asked excitedly.

"A traveler stopped by the ranger station and reported that a young elk had been struck by a car at the game crossing and left injured beside the road. I went to look at it and put it out of its misery, but I found it not to be so badly injured as to warrant killing it. It has a hip injury and a bad cut on its neck, both of which will heal in time. But the herd has gone on and left it, and alone in the wilds with no protection, it would die. I'd like to leave it here so I can tend its injuries and have you care for it until it is able to be returned to the herd."

Ronnie climbed up on the truck and looked at the elk. Why, it wasn't a regal-looking creature with spreading antlers! It was just a baby, not much bigger than a young colt, and it had no horns at all!

"Do you mean it isn't against the law for us to keep it?" asked Ronnie, remembering all that Mr. Mallow had said about folks keeping wild creatures in captivity.

"It isn't, since I am authorizing you to do so, but only until it is well enough to return to the wilds, you understand. It is definitely against the law for individuals to capture and pen an elk. But this one was not captured, nor will he be penned, and you will be performing an act of mercy to keep him now that he is injured and lost from the herd."

"Have you named him yet?" Ronnie asked.

"Of course not," Mr. Mallow laughed. "I got him only an hour ago. But you can name him if you wish."

"Well, does he belong to the lodge?" asked Ronnie.

"The lodge? What lodge?" asked the puzzled Mr. Mallow.

"Why, the Elk lodge that all the elks belong to," explained Ronnie, surprised that Mr. Mallow didn't know.

"Animals don't belong to the lodge, son." Daddy laughed. "People do. The elk is their symbol."

Ronnie laughed at the joke on himself. "Well, for a long time people have been naming their lodge for the elk, now it's time an elk was named for their lodge. Let's name him 'Lodge.' "

Even though injured and in pain, the young elk fought against going into the barn. With everybody helping, they finally got the animal inside and put him in a stall near Drifter. Mr. Mallow and Daddy tended his cuts, fed and watered him, and then covered him with a blanket.

"When he is well again, and we free him, it would be interesting if we marked him, so that we can follow his activities in the wilds," Daddy said. "Would that be possible?"

"Oh, yes. We frequently mark animals, and band birds, so that we can learn more about their range and feeding and other habits."

The nasty cuts soon healed, leaving hardly any scars at all, and by the time they were healed Lodge was a pet. Being very young, he had quickly adapted himself to the ways of domestic life and to the people who had treated him kindly.

The burro and the two milk goats Columbine and Faun, whom Daddy had bought to assist Ronnie in being a Future Farmer of America, became Lodge's friends, as did Drifter. As soon as Lodge was freed from the barn he tagged around after the other animals as if he had always belonged with them. It seemed to Ronnie that the little elk who loved carrots, apples, and lump sugar was growing very fast. And it seemed to Ronnie, also, that the young creature didn't know that he was an elk, or that he was supposed to be wild. He showed no desire or inclination to return to the wilderness. He was utterly content on Tattercoat Range, and Ronnie couldn't understand why he shouldn't remain there if he wanted to.

"Elk and deer are very gentle when young, but the bucks, especially when adult, sometimes grow very dangerous and often attack people. No, son, we must take Lodge back to his kind and let him run freely and happily," Daddy said.

Several times they did take Lodge, leading him by a rope, into the forest miles from home. And time and again they did succeed in leaving him there. Sometimes he would stay for the remainder of the day, but that evening he would be back at the barn door, crying to be let in with his other friends.

He didn't want to be wild. He liked being with people better, and being fed apples and carrots, and particularly lump sugar. But Daddy said that they must keep returning him to the forest, until the time came when he would decide to stay.

Ronnie went out to the barn where Daddy was working. He saw a long rod with a strange design on its end in his hand. It was the outline of a merry-go-round horse, the symbol of Tattercoat Range.

"Oh, Daddy, you're not going to monogram Drifter's hide, are you? You will spoil his coat. He is so beautiful."

Daddy laughed. "You mean brand. No, I'm not going to brand Drifter. As you say, he is much too beautiful to brand. I am going to have the inside of one of his ears tattooed, however, so that if he ever becomes lost or is stolen, we can claim him. But I am going to brand Lodge today. You remember we talked about it when we first got him, and decided that we would like to follow his activities and movements on the range when he returns to the herd and runs wild again."

Lodge, curious as usual, didn't know what was in store for him as he stood watching Daddy heat the branding iron. Tiny nubbins that would grow into antlers were beginning to sprout on his head. He was growing up.

Daddy turned the iron in the coals until it was white-hot, then slapped it against Lodge's hip, and there, outlined for as long as Lodge's beautiful hide should last, was the symbol of Tattercoat Range.

Daddy smeared salve on the brand to relieve the burning. "Now, Ronnie, we're going to take Lodge far away, much farther than we have taken him before. This time he will stay with the herd."

So they led Lodge far, far away, where the shining peaks seemed almost near, and where the elk herd ran.

Daddy removed the rope from around his neck, slapped the hip that wasn't branded, and shooed Lodge into the timber where the herd were grazing.

Lodge looked back at them, and at Drifter, his friend too. Then he looked toward the mysterious herd of which he had once been a member. It seemed as

though he did not wish to join those strange yet somehow familiar creatures. He would rather stay with the people and the animals who were his friends on Tattercoat Range.

The herd moved slowly forward, nibbling the luxuriant grass. Another yearling looked quizzically toward Lodge. Lodge moved on young, hesistant, but curious feet, toward him.

Ronnie and Daddy, looking back over their shoulders as they began the descent toward home, saw Lodge approach the edge of the herd. The other elk looked at him in a mildly curious way.

Then something startled the herd, perhaps a mountain lion on the hunt, and with almost a single motion they dashed on flashing hoofs to the uplands.

And Lodge went right along with them.

10

The DANCING DOLL *and* LAZARUS

Who Arose from the Dead

THE LETTER sounded very legal and impressive. Daddy and Mother read and reread it. Ronnie couldn't understand all the legal phrases, so Daddy explained it to him.

A man whom Daddy had never seen, and had never known, had died, leaving his entire estate, including the dancing doll, to Daddy. The man's name had been O'Leary too, and having no relatives of his own, he had searched the country for someone named O'Leary whom he could trust to receive his estate. He had made inquiries about Daddy and learned that he was a good, kind man, and so made a will, leaving his entire worldly goods to Lance O'Leary. The letter was from a lawyer, telling Daddy of Mr. O'Leary's death and informing him that the dancing doll would be delivered to Tattercoat Range that day, and that he would arrive to explain things more fully, deliver a check, and have Daddy sign release papers.

"A dancing doll?" cried Mother. "That is a strange thing for a man to leave in his estate, saying that it is his most valued possession. I wonder how big the doll is. It must be one of those valuable handmade dolls that dance when wound up. I have heard of some costing as much as several thousand dollars. And to think the man left you all of his money as well, without knowing you, or ever having seen you."

"Maybe the doll is a puppet," Ronnie suggested, "that dances when you pull strings."

"Well, we won't have long to wonder. The letter says the doll is to be delivered today, and that the lawyer who is settling the estate will be here this afternoon," said Mother.

Daddy was quite excited about being left money and a valuable dancing doll. He didn't know what they would do with the doll, but since the dead man had valued it so highly he would respect the trust.

Daddy had gone to the post office to mail some illustrations, so he wasn't home when Ronnie came running in to tell Mother that the dancing doll must be arriving, for he heard a truck turning off the highway and coming up the lane.

The big truck at last came into view. Mother and Ronnie were standing in Timothy Tattercoat's garden, eager to see the dancing doll.

"Why, Ronnie, that truck isn't bringing a doll. That's a stock truck, and it's hauling a horse. Now don't tell me Daddy has bought another horse and forgotten to mention it."

"Where do you want this horse put, lady?" one of the men called from the truck.

"Well, I don't know. Are you sure you are at the right place? My husband didn't say anything about a horse."

"The name is O'Leary, isn't it? Lance O'Leary?"

"Yes," said Mother.

"Well, this is the right place then. The address on this paper says 'Lance O'Leary, Tattercoat Range,' and the sign up over the gate by the highway says this is Tattercoat Range."

"Well, I guess then that there's no mistake," Mother said. "I can't understand why my husband didn't mention that a horse was being delivered today. You'd better take it to the barn and put it in a stall until Mr. O'Leary decides about it."

The men unloaded the horse and drove away after Mother signed the receipt.

Daddy came in about lunch time. Had the lawyer come yet, he asked, and had the dancing doll been delivered?

"No," said Mother. "But two men brought the

horse you bought and forgot to mention. It's in the barn."

"Horse?" said Daddy. "I didn't buy any horse!"

"Are you sure, Lance? The name on the delivery slip said 'Lance O'Leary, Tattercoat Range.'"

"Well, I sure didn't buy any horse and then forget about it," snorted Daddy. "Did you have to pay any money?"

"No," said Mother. "They said everything was already taken care of."

Daddy and Ronnie went to the barn, where Mr. Paulsen was currying the big white horse.

"This is a nice horse, Mr. O'Leary," said Mr. Paulsen. "But why did you buy such an old one? Why this horse must be over twenty years old. Her teeth are worn off. She's not going to be good for much work."

"I didn't buy it," Daddy explained again. "I don't know anything about it. It's just as much a mystery to me as it is to you."

"There is a small bundle of things over in the corner which the delivery men left with the horse — said it belonged to her. You want to open it?" Mr. Paulsen suggested.

"I haven't time now. It's lunch time, and the lawyer will soon be here from Denver. I'll see about it later."

After lunch the lawyer arrived and was invited into

the living room, where Mother had coffee and cake waiting.

"My, you do love animals, don't you?" smiled the lawyer, looking at the dogs, cat, and coon. "Has the Dancing Doll been delivered yet?"

"No," Daddy said. "We have been expecting it all day, but it hasn't arrived."

"That's strange. The truck left Denver before daylight this morning."

"Well, it hasn't been delivered here. Nothing has been delivered all day except a mysterious old white horse which I didn't buy."

"A big white horse?" queried the lawyer. "Why, that's the Dancing Doll."

"I don't understand — " Daddy said feebly.

"Well, I'll explain," said the lawyer.

His client, Danny O'Leary, had made inquiries before his death to find an O'Leary who lived on a ranch or in the country, loved animals, who would be kind to his old horse — Dancing Doll — and give her a good home for the remainder of her life. The man was also leaving all of his money to take care of Dancing Doll, for she wasn't charity.

"You see, Danny O'Leary was a very old man. He had been a circus clown, and when he left the circus five years ago because of ill health he retired his trick horse along with himself. He lived quietly on an acreage at the edge of Denver. The Dancing Doll was his only family. He wished to make provision for her, and that is how you came into the picture. If you refuse to accept her, there is nothing to do but send her to the rendering plant, for she is too old to be used for working."

"Oh, we wouldn't do that!" said Daddy. "We've plenty of room here, and she will not be any trouble at all. I understand how that old circus clown felt. We wouldn't want our animals to be sent to a rendering plant or to the pound. If anything happened to us, we would want someone to give them good homes. And of all creatures in the world, it seems that an old circus horse who has spent her entire life making other people happy should have a peaceful old age."

"Mr. O'Leary thought you would feel that way; that's why he named you in his will. He found out how much you love animals, and how much room you have."

"How about all that money the man left?" chimed in Ronnie.

"I'm coming to that," smiled the lawyer. "Danny O'Leary left you all his money, it is true, and at the time he made his will he had a nice little nest egg, but bills and long illness cut it down. After funeral expenses were paid, I'm afraid there is practically nothing left. Here is your check."

Daddy looked at the check. The amount written on it was one hundred and one dollars.

"I'm afraid it's hardly enough to make it worth your time and trouble," the lawyer continued.

"It doesn't matter," Daddy said, smiling. "I've never inherited any money before, and this is a big surprise. In fact everything about it has been most surprising. We expected a mechanical doll, and we got a horse. This will be ample to pay for all of Dolly's expenses for the rest of her life, and if there had been nothing left at all, we would still give Dolly a good home. She's welcome here."

"I had hoped you'd feel that way," smiled the lawyer. "She's a nice, gentle old horse and she misses her kind master. She remembers many of her old circus tricks, and I'm sure you will enjoy her. She can jump through a burning hoop and do many other things, but mostly she was known for her dance steps, and so was named 'Dolly, the Dancing Horse,' later shortened to the 'Dancing Doll.' Her circus equipment should have been delivered along with her."

"Yes." Daddy smiled. "It's in the barn, but I haven't opened it yet, so I don't know what's in it. Let's go out there, shall we?"

Dolly greeted them with whinnies of joy.

Daddy unrolled the bundle and displayed a number of faded circus pamphlets announcing in large red letters, "Danny, the Clown, and his performing horse, the Dancing Doll." There were also bracelets of small bells to be put on Dolly's ankles when she danced to the tune of "Jingle Bells," a satin blanket with her name on it, and red and gold tassels for her ears. These were all of Dolly's earthly goods.

"Wow!" gasped Ronnie, "A real performing circus horse, right here on Tattercoat Range."

Mr. Paulsen, who had been listening quietly, went into his little house and returned with his violin. Daddy fastened the bracelets of bells around Dolly's front ankles, and when Mr. Paulsen started playing "Jingle Bells" she pranced and raised her feet gracefully, keeping time to the music. When he switched to "The Beautiful Blue Danube," Dolly went into a waltz. She was a versatile horse, and was patted and given lumps of sugar for her performance.

"Well, I'm glad old Dolly has such a wonderful home where she can spend her remaining years," the lawyer said as he climbed into his car and drove away.

"Now we have two circus horses!" Ronnie exclaimed.

"Two? What do you mean?" asked Mother.

"Have you forgotten that Timothy Tattercoat was once a circus horse?" Ronnie asked.

"Why, that's right!" said Mother. "He certainly was."

A few days later Ronnie, Daddy, and Mother were driving through the big gate which marked the entrance to their property. A car was stopped beside the highway, beside which were standing three children crying as though their hearts would break.

"Need some help?" Daddy asked the driver.

"No thanks. Had a blowout, but it's fixed now."

"Why are your children crying?" Ronnie asked.

"While I was changing the tire, the dog got out of the car and was killed by a car speeding around the curve. We thought a heap of that little mongrel. They want to bury him. Do you think it will be all right to bury him here alongside the road?"

"I'm sorry about your dog," Daddy said sympathetically. "I'll tell you what — our place is just up this road, and we have a pet cemetery in the pine grove behind the house. Why not take your dog up there and bury him? Mr. Paulsen, who will probably be around the barn, will loan you a spade. It will be more comfort for your children to know that their pet is

resting in a pet cemetery instead of beside the highway."

"Thanks a lot," said the man, lifting the body of a
small, fuzzy, grayish dog into the car.

"I'll go back with them and help," Ronnie said. "I
don't need to go to town anyway."

He got into the car beside the children and pointed
out the cemetery to them. Then he got the spade and
helped dig a deep grave into which the body of the
little dog was placed. They all tamped the earth
thoroughly and placed rocks on top, to keep wild animals from digging into the fresh-made grave. The children gathered a small bunch of wild flowers and left
them there.

That night the O'Learys were sitting around pop-
ping corn and listening to Mr. Mallow tell stories. In
the midst of one of the most exciting stories about a
grizzly bear, there was a faint scratching sound at the
door. Daddy opened it.

There lay a small dog, covered with blood and moist
earth.

"A car has hit him. His hind leg and tail are broken,
and he has a head injury. This highway is getting very
bad. This is the second dog hit here today," Daddy
said.

"Why, that's the dog that was killed and buried to-day!" Ronnie said in amazement.

"Are you sure, Ronnie?"

"I ought to be. I helped bury him."

"I think your are right. This dog has a head wound which would have left him unconscious for a long time, and make him appear dead, and he certainly looks as if he had been buried. He's covered with dirt."

"He dug out of his grave!" cried Ronnie. "And that grave was tamped down and had rocks piled on it! Think of how he must have felt when he came to and found himself buried alive."

"Poor little fellow," said Mr. Mallow. "Mind if I take him along with me, Lance? He needs some expert medical attention. I'll take him over to Herb's hospital and have his leg and tail set, and his other wounds tended. Perhaps there's a chance he will recover. I'll see if I can find the dog's owners."

"The car had an Oklahoma license plate, but how would you ever locate it?"

"I don't know, but I can try," and Mr. Mallow gently lifted the dog into a blanket to take him to Ralph's brother Herb's "hospital." "If I don't find his owners, I'll keep him and give him a good home. I don't have a dog now since Rip was killed by the mountain lion."

For the next few days Mr. Mallow had an announcement broadcast over the Denver radio station, but evidently the Oklahoma car did not have a radio or had got too far away. The dog was never claimed, so Mr. Mallow kept him.

"What are you going to name him?" Ronnie asked.

"What do you think?" Mr. Mallow smiled, rubbing the dog's shaggy ears. "You go to Sunday School, Ronnie — do you know your Bible?"

"Pretty well," admitted Ronnie.

"Well, then perhaps you remember the story of Lazarus who arose from the dead. That is almost what this dog did, so I am going to call him Lazarus."

"Listen!" said Ronnie. "The scissors-grinder man is down on the highway. Hear his music?"

The tinkling notes of a calliope came through the morning air to the gray house on Tattercoat Range.

"Here are our scissors and knives, Ronnie," Mother said. "Take them down to the highway to be sharpened. Now where in the world does Dolly think she is going?"

Dolly had pushed open the gate and was trotting eagerly down the lane toward the highway. The notes of the calliope filling the forest lured her on. Circus music! Circus music! Dolly could hardly believe her ears. Memories were awakened.

When Ronnie reached the highway with his knives and scissors there was Dolly prancing around the funny old wagon, dancing to the music of the calliope.

11

LADDIE *Repays His Debt*

LADDIE WAS the kindest, gentlest, shyest dog the O'Learys had ever known. He seemed to be eternally grateful to them for having saved his life and given him a home. He loved each member of the household, and Mitzi most of all. Perhaps he admired the little poodle's lack of fear, because Laddie always remained a little shy and frightened at things he didn't understand. Sometimes Ronnie thought he was the most cowardly dog who ever lived. He stood in awe of everything that flew, walked, ran, crawled, or moved at all. The chipmunks startled him. The bluejays terrified him. Strange people caused him to run and hide in the kitchen even before they spoke a word. However, when he did become friends with something or someone, he more or less emerged from his shell of fear, although he never would really be brave. If anyone spoke sharply, or raised a hand suddenly, even for some harmless purpose, he would crouch and cower in fear.

Daddy said Laddie's behavior was the result of the cruel treatment the dog had suffered before he came to Tattercoat Range. Poor Laddie could never quite forget it.

Ronnie was thinking about Laddie when Daddy interrupted saying, "I owe the publishers at least a dozen illustrations. With all the mouths I have to feed, I can't remain idle long. We're going on a field trip today, Ronnie. No pigs, coons, cats, or dogs are eligible for this trip, but I have no objection to one small boy tagging along."

"Where are we going, Daddy?" Ronnie asked, though it didn't matter. Any place they went would be wonderful. It was early morning. Dew covered the earth and Drifter pawed the ground, eager to be off. Mother had given them sandwiches, potato salad, and sliced cake to take.

"About eight miles up that mountain." Daddy pointed. "There is a big beaver dam. I need some beaver pictures."

Drifter hardly seemed to walk. He appeared to be treading on air, his silver mane floating in the breeze, his neck arched, and his coat dappled with sunshine and shadow. Drifter certainly was a king among horses.

Ronnie was thinking how desolate the dogs had

looked as Mother held them back. Their eyes, pleading and wistful, had followed Ronnie, Daddy, and Drifter. They had wanted to go so badly; but they would frighten the animals and Daddy wouldn't get his pictures.

When the way became steep and rocky, they dismounted and led Drifter. The forest closed in upon them, primitive and still, with great trees dark against the sky, and grass deep and green. The bushes were covered with blossoms and berries. They could hear the roar of the river, and above them a waterfall sparkled in the sun, its water foaming into the river below.

Suddenly Daddy stopped and nudged Ronnie. He pointed to a bush a few feet away, then put his finger to his lips for silence. Ronnie looked and looked, but nothing stirred. He saw only some brown leaves beneath the bush, with white spots where the sun touched them. Not even a blade of grass moved. But as he looked more carefully, he saw two brown eyes looking at him, and suddenly the brown and white spots took on form, and Ronnie knew that he was looking at a tiny fawn. Eagerly he started toward it.

"No," whispered Daddy. "Don't go near it. Its mother has hidden it there. She may be off feeding, or perhaps she is leading some enemy away from it. The little fawn knows that its very life depends on remaining absolutely motionless and not attracting attention to itself. If a human touches it, its mother will not take it back. Many fawns have been left motherless because most people do not know this. It is no kindness to take one home with you, unless you know that its mother is dead. Always remember that, and never touch a fawn that you may think has been abandoned."

They had left the river and the waterfall, and now all was silent again except for the chirping and fluttering of birds, and the distant hammering of a woodpecker on a pine tree. These important birds served as exterminators of the forest, ridding the trees of bugs and borers.

Ronnie and Daddy stopped to let Drifter "blow" after the steep climb, and poured hot drinks from the thermos. Daddy was looking back down the trail over which they had come. Suddenly he took his gun from the saddle sheath, the gun which he always carried, but almost never used.

"There is something following us along the trail. I thought so a while ago, and now I'm sure. Maybe it is a cougar. Sit still."

Drifter looked down the trail and snorted. Ronnie could now hear something pat-pat-pattering on the earth and stones. Suddenly around the bend appeared a familiar object. It saw them watching, and sat down.

Swishing his tail eagerly, he turned his head first to one side, then to the other, looking wistful. It was Laddie, a little doubtful of his reception.

"Laddie, why must you be so dumb?" Ronnie cried. "Daddy said you had to stay home."

"And he did — until he found a chance to slip away and follow us. He had some trailing to do. Well, after all, he was bred for trailing and hunting."

"Well, he sure won't scare the animals. Laddie couldn't scare anything."

Laddie crawled forward on his stomach, a question in his eyes.

"Okay, come on, Lad," Daddy said gently.

Laddie rushed forward and greeted them as if he hadn't seen them for a week.

"You're a bad dog," Daddy said, stroking the long, silky ears. "But since you're here, you'll have to come with us. We can't have you wandering around by yourself in the woods."

It wasn't a very enthusiastic invitation, but Laddie didn't seem to know the difference, although he was trying hard to make up for his badness, trotting along at their side, looking neither to the left nor to the right. He would never have chased anything anyway because of the fear that it would turn on him. Drifter was glad to see him, for they were the best of friends.

Now they came to a smaller stream and followed it up the mountainside. A water ousel flitted into the water for food, swaying and dipping its body with the movement of the water.

Slap, slap, came a sound from up above.

"That sound comes from the beaver dam," Daddy explained. "The sentinel beaver has heard us and is warning the others by slapping his flat tail on the water."

Directly ahead of them lay a small meadow, in the center of which was a little pond with deep green grass growing around its edges. Many of the aspen trees around the clearing had been cut, but none of the evergreens. Daddy explained that the beavers had cut down the aspens, but wouldn't touch the evergreens because they didn't like the taste of the resin in the wood. He called them the world's original lumbermen because they have been using trees for building and food for millions of years. Daddy pointed to an aspen which was almost gnawed through. Their approach had probably interrupted the beavers' work on it. As a rule beavers gnaw all the way around a tree until it falls, then they roll and drag the trunks and branches into the water, plaster them with mud to dam up the stream and make a pond, then they form their lodges. The bark they store away for winter food. The many humplike structures which Ronnie had noticed in the pond were the beavers' lodges.

Daddy had staked Drifter down the hill so the beavers wouldn't hear him. Then he and Ronnie sat down very quietly, and Daddy unpacked his sketch pad and camera. Laddie lay at their feet, hardly moving.

They had come to this distant pond because the beavers worked in the daytime. Here they were seldom disturbed by people, and guns and traps were unknown to them. Farther down, closer to civilization, beavers worked only at night.

Ronnie watched a happy little green-and-yellow goldfinch sitting on a thistle, singing to its mate on the nest in a nearby thicket. Suddenly the bird swooped on a bug and carried it to the nest.

"I'm hungry," whispered Ronnie.

"It's only ten o'clock, but we'll eat if you're hungry," Daddy whispered. Daddy believed in letting people eat when they were hungry, not just when the clock said it was time.

The little pond lay silent and still, not a beaver in sight. Ronnie wondered if Daddy wasn't mistaken about the beaver colony still living here. Maybe they had migrated, as he knew they sometimes did.

The ham sandwiches and potato salad tasted wonderful, and so did the thick slices of chocolate cake.

"Action," whispered Daddy, "is a very important part of life and brings much happiness. There is compensation, however, in being able to sit quietly and watch and wait. People who can't do this, and who have no patience, miss much, indeed." Daddy wouldn't even light his pipe for fear the beavers would smell it.

Ronnie was beginning to believe that he was one of the people who would "miss much, indeed," for he was growing most impatient.

Then there was a ripple across the little pond, and a dark head, like that of a giant rat, could be seen.

"They think it is safe to come out now," Daddy whispered.

Laddie pricked up his ears, but Ronnie placed a hand on his head so that he couldn't move.

"Down," ordered Daddy, and for a wonder Laddie sank back against the log.

Soon other heads appeared on the pond, followed by splashes and the queer sounds of the beavers talking to each other.

"Everything has its own communication system. Animals talk to each other in their own way. Not so that we can understand them, perhaps, but that isn't important as long as they can understand each other," Daddy said.

A big beaver started gnawing on the tree that was almost eaten through. Others gathered sticks and carried them to the pond.

"They work all spring, summer, and fall, getting ready for the winter," Daddy went on. "Getting ready for the time when the water freezes and food is scarce. A great portion of the lodge is beneath the water, but fresh air can still reach it. The beavers store their supplies down there, and live in safety when the pond is frozen. Deep down the water doesn't freeze, and the beavers can swim out if necessary."

"If they live under the water, why do people say that forest fires harm them?"

"Because the trees, their food supply, are destroyed, and the water polluted. The beavers who survive move to a new location, sometimes to an already established colony, where they are welcomed by the settlers who seem to understand their need."

Ronnie finished the last of his cake and gave Laddie a bite.

Daddy continued, now sketching rapidly. "Beavers are builders, architects, and lumbermen, and do not know the meaning of idleness. They are very different from the gay, carefree otters who live on Tattercoat Range. Beavers can change the courses of rivers or streams, and in areas where they are trapped and destroyed much land is washed away. Their pelts are soft and heavy, and highly prized. We never allow trapping up here, so this colony has grown, and some have moved to a new location, and are now making a new pond higher up in the mountains."

A few baby beavers came up on the bank and played like kittens or puppies. Their mothers watched the play.

"See their broad, heavy, flat tails?" Daddy asked. "When that tail hits the water it causes the slapping sound you heard a while ago. It is a warning signal, and like the Indian drums it carries many different messages."

The aspen suddenly fell, and for a moment Ronnie was startled. Laddie almost jumped out of his skin. Several of the larger beavers hurried to the fallen tree, and with their big, sharp, yellow teeth tore at the bark and branches.

Ronnie watched the activity with much interest. He was certainly glad that there would never be any traps in Tattercoat Range or in the beaver dam. The thing that fascinated him most about the animals was the intelligence of their communication system.

Daddy finished one sketch and started another. "If you're tired of sitting, you and Laddie can explore a bit. Go downhill, so the beavers won't notice you. Use your emergency whistle if anything goes wrong, and don't go far."

They walked quietly until the beavers could no longer hear them.

The ground was littered with bright, shining, silvery stones — mica like the stones in Grandmother Tayton's fireplace, light in weight and thin. There were many other interesting stones, some of which Ronnie gathered for his collection. He dug for Timothy's garden a particularly beautiful flower that looked like a small orchid, and put it in the damp bank of the stream to keep it fresh. He would get it before they left for home.

He watched a mother bluejay feeding her young. The father jay swooped and scolded at Laddie, who was terrified, so they went on their way. A kingfisher dived into the stream and emerged with a struggling trout.

On the hillside, almost hidden by the bushes, Ronnie saw a hole. It had a timber frame and looked like a well turned on its side. An old rusty broken pick lay in the earth. Someone must have dug there, perhaps hunting for silver.

A chipmunk scurried into the opening, so Ronnie

knew there were no dangerous animals inside, or the chipmunk wouldn't have gone in. Suddenly he, too, had an overwhelming desire to see what was inside. He paid no attention to the still, small voice that warned him against it. He and Laddie crawled inside the opening. It was very dark so he switched on the flashlight which he always carried in his belt when on an outing. The opening wasn't very deep. He could plainly see the end of it, and there was nothing there, not even the chipmunk. Maybe he could find a little piece of silver for his collection, and point to it proudly saying that he alone had discovered it.

There were timbers bracing the walls and roof, and it looked very safe. Certainly there was nothing to hurt anyone. There were no poisonous snakes in this high altitude. They went farther into the mine, Laddie reluctantly, looking longingly toward the opening. Ronnie called him an old sissy.

He dug into the side of the mine with the point of his knife until he hit a rock and dug it out. Maybe, when it was washed he would see silver in it.

Laddie kept edging toward the opening.

"Laddie, you're an old coward, afraid of your own shadow."

The dog looked as if he knew it, but couldn't help it.

They were starting out when Ronnie slipped and

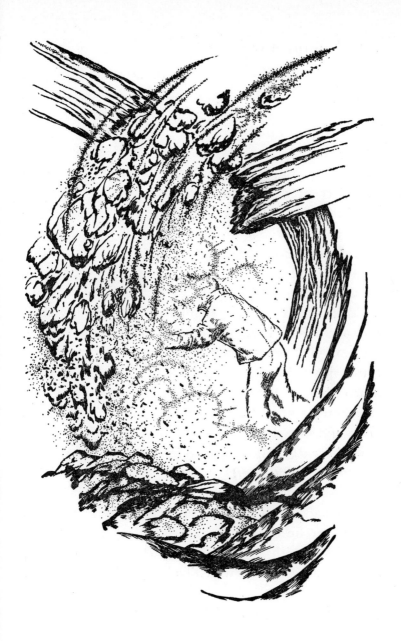

fell against one of the timbers. It was old and rotten, and it broke. There was a grinding, crashing noise, and dirt, stones, and timbers fell into the mine. The air was full of dust.

Laddie jumped and yelped, and tore for the opening. He made it, but Ronnie did not. When he got there it was covered over. He pushed and dug with his pocket knife, but to no avail. He was sealed in the old mine and no one in the world knew where he was. Back at the beaver dam Daddy would wait for a while, then call and call, and finally hunt for him, but he would never find him.

Faintly he could hear Laddie whining outside, and now and then a bark, but soon there was only silence. He was glad he had his flashlight. Even though it could not help him to get out, he wasn't nearly so much afraid as he would have been in the pitch-dark. He thought of the whistle on the chain around his neck, and blew hard on it. But he knew Daddy could never hear it, coming from so far inside the earth. No one could hear it ever.

Tears ran down his face. He was more afraid now than he had ever been in his entire life. He had known really that he shouldn't have gone inside the mine and wished with all his heart that he had paid attention to that wee voice which had warned him. If even

Laddie were here with him, it wouldn't be quite so bad, but Laddie was safe. He was glad that Laddie didn't have to share the fate of being sealed in an abandoned mine. He wished too that he had paid attention to Laddie, who hadn't wanted to go inside at all, and had shivered and trembled when they were inside. He wished he hadn't called Laddie a coward.

A long time passed. He didn't know how long a time, but it seemed an eternity. He thought of Mother, who would miss him. But wait, was that a bark he heard? Then he heard it again, and was sure. Laddie hadn't abandoned him after all. He had come back. Then he heard Daddy's voice, very distant.

"Ronnie! Son! Can you hear me?"

"Yes," yelled Ronnie.

"Sit very still, Ronnie," came the faint voice. "Don't move around. I'll try to get you out myself, but if I have to go for help, try not to be afraid, and remember to sit very quietly so as not to cause any more earth to cave in. Can you hear me?"

"Yes," Ronnie answered, "and I'm not afraid any more."

He sat down, as Daddy had told him to do, away from the entrance. He knew that a person had to have fresh air to be able to live, and he wondered how long the air would last. He wondered if taking little, tiny breaths would help, but found that awfully hard to do.

He had turned off the flashlight to save the battery and put it down. If Daddy had to go for help, he would be entirely alone again. It was different with Daddy just outside. He reached for his flashlight, but it wasn't there. He started to crawl around and hunt for it, but remembered what Daddy had said, so sat very still.

He could hear Daddy digging with the camp shovel which they always carried on trips. He heard Laddie barking and whining. After what seemed a very long time he could hear Daddy moving rocks away, and then he saw a tiny beam of light. The light grew bigger and stronger, and the hole grew larger, but still he didn't move until Daddy said, "Now, son, take it easy. Don't get excited and don't hurry. Above all, don't touch those timbers. Move slowly and crawl out. I think you can make it. If the earth starts falling, just lie flat and cover your head with your arm."

His feet kicked his flashlight, so he retrieved it and put it inside his shirt. Then he did exactly as Daddy had told him, and crawled out of the hole. He heard falling earth behind him, but he was outside before the mine caved in completely.

How good that fresh air smelled!

Laddie was licking his face. Ronnie was glad of that so Daddy wouldn't know about the tears. Then Daddy grabbed him and hugged him very hard, and felt him all over to see if he was hurt, which he wasn't. He handed him a candy bar, and poured coffee from the kit.

"Oh, Daddy, I'm ashamed. I was afraid and I cried a little bit. I wasn't going to tell you because Laddie licked the tears off and I didn't want you to know that I'm not very brave."

"Anyone in the world would have been afraid in that spot. No one except a fool is never afraid. You shouldn't have gone inside that old mine, Ronnie, but you know that. I think you've been punished enough. If the mine had been bigger, it is possible that no one could have rescued you. Don't ever do anything like that again."

Daddy's face was sort of gray, as though he were sick, and he was almost as dirty as Ronnie.

Laddie continued to jump all over Ronnie on the way to the stream.

"I thought you had run away and left me all alone, Laddie," Ronnie said, washing the dirt off, and collecting the stones and flowers from the bank.

"I would never have found you, or known what happened to you if it hadn't been for old Lad," Daddy said. "He came back to me, barking and trying to get me to follow him. He kept running ahead and looking back at me, and led me to the mine. No one could have mistaken his meaning. I couldn't have found you without Laddie because the falling earth and rocks had covered your footprints. And time was so important."

Laddie seemed grateful for all the praise that was being heaped upon him, and for the bite of candy which he received.

"Do you know what?" asked Daddy. "Laddie made so much noise that he frightened all the beavers to the bottom of the pond. I'll bet they won't come out until tomorrow."

"Laddie has a communication system, too," Ronnie said, stroking Laddie's long, silky ears, wet on the tips because he had drunk from the stream. "Yes, sir! Laddie has a good communication system, and he's smart and brave."

Laddie's eyes shone, and his thumping stubby tail pounded the mud.

12

DOT-'N'-DASH,

the Fremont Squirrel,

and LITTLE STINKER

F OR SOME TIME Mother had been wistfully saying that never had the orphan box been empty so long.

But that was soon remedied.

Mother had gone over to Mrs. Drake's to take her some plants and come back with a squirrel — as if the forest was not full enough of squirrels.

This one was different. It was a tiny gray Fremont, or spruce, squirrel with a bushy, lacy tail and tufted ears. All Fremont squirrels are small, but this one was no bigger than a chipmunk. It had fallen from a high branch of a tree when it was very young, injuring some gland and causing its growth to be stunted. From that time on it had lived in Mrs. Drake's woodpile, becoming very tame. Just recently a large piece of stove wood had fallen on the little fellow, breaking one of its forelegs. Mother had brought the squirrel home so that it could rest safely in the orphan box while the needle-size bone set.

Now that the squirrel had completely recovered, he no longer stayed in the orphan box. He stayed every-place except out of doors with the other squirrels. They were so much bigger than he that they terrified him, and, like Trader Horn, he found various ways to get back in again.

Mother named him Dot-'N'-Dash because he was not much bigger than a dot and he dashed all over the place. He had one upsetting habit of dashing across the room, lunging for one of the shade cords, and then swinging from it to some other section of the room. Mother was continually startled every time he appeared in some unexpected place, swinging in front of her face.

It was Mother who discovered another habit that he acquired one morning when she was powdering her face. She dipped the big fluffy puff into her crystal powder jar, and was about to pat her face with it when she discovered that Dot-'N'-Dash had been using her powder jar as his bathroom.

"Did you ever hear of anything so terrible?" she fumed, dumping the powder out and locking the re-filled jar in a drawer. "I'll break him of that habit right now. I'll put the jar where he can't get to it."

Everything was fine for an hour or so, when Daddy started to fill his pipe. Dot-'N'-Dash had taken over

the tobacco jar for his new bathroom.

"For crying out loud!" Daddy bellowed. "He couldn't possibly have found a worse place."

"Oh, yes, he could," Mother said. "He could have decided on the sugar bowl."

"Or the cookie jar," Ronnie chimed in.

"That reminds me," Daddy said, changing the subject. "Do you know what became of the bucket of sand I had sitting in that warm place just above the pipes?"

"Why, yes. I set it outside the day before yesterday. It was just sand, wasn't it?" Mother looked up from preparing lunch.

"It was sand all right, but it was desert sand covering five eggs which I hoped would hatch out in the warm pantry. The nights are so cool outside that the eggs won't hatch now."

"Oh, I'm sorry," said Mother. "What kind of eggs were they?"

"Gila monster eggs," Daddy said sadly. "I brought them back from the desert last month to see if I could hatch them in this high altitude."

"Gila monster eggs! Aren't Gila monsters poisonous?"

"Yes, but I didn't intend to keep them. I just wanted

to make the test, and then give the small Gila monsters to the Denver zoo."

"Now, you listen to me, Lance O'Leary. I don't mind trade rats any more. And I've reached the place where I don't mind raising wood mice in the coffee can in the window. I don't mind feeding all the squirrels, chipmunks, and birds in the forest. I don't mind wild deer and elk, and horses and cats and dogs — or even Fremont squirrels. I don't mind coons or pigs, or any of the other strange things you and Ronnie bring home for me to doctor, nurse, raise on bottles, scrub and tend. But I do mind Gila monsters in my pantry."

"Now, honey, you don't understand. A naturalist has to make such tests if he wants to know all about things in nature," Daddy said patiently.

"Not in this house, and not in this pantry, you don't. If you want to start raising Gila monsters, you will just have to do so in the barn."

"It's too cold there. They have to have the same temperature they would have on the warm desert."

"Well, we'll discuss it later. Rosy Glow is out of her pen again. Listen to all that noise."

After Rosy Glow had been chased back into her pen, Mother discovered that she had no sugar, so she sent Ronnie over to Ralph's house to borrow some. He returned with Ralph, having completely forgotten to ask for the sugar. He had something much more exciting than mere sugar.

"I've something for you, Mother. Guess what?" he said, reaching into his deep pocket, which obviously held a squirming, living occupant.

"Oh, Ronald! Not another pig. I'm wise to you and your surprises. Not something else for me to raise on a bottle?"

"Now, Mother, you know I couldn't bring another pig home, even if Rosy Glow did turn out so well. You like her pretty well yourself. You said you would feel like a cannibal if you ate one bite of her, because she calls you Mother."

"Well, what is it this time? I guess I'm fortified for anything."

Ronnie withdrew his hand from his big handy pocket, pulling out a small black-and-white-striped skunk.

"Oh!" shrieked Mother, jumping up on the kitchen chair. "I'm not fortified for that. It will smell up the entire place."

Daddy burst out laughing.

"Mother," Ronnie said pityingly, "I know better than that. Do you think I'd put an ordinary skunk in my pocket?"

"I don't know," Mother said. "You've put every-thing else in there."

"If I may continue," said Ronnie patiently, "I was about to say that this little skunk has been de-skunked. Ralph's brother performed a minor operation on it; so there is no danger of its skunking up the place."

Mother jumped down from the chair.

"Well," she said briskly, "why didn't you say so? Honestly, Ronnie, if you would just explain to people instead of barging in here like this, pulling skunks out of your pocket!"

The little skunk kept very still and quiet, unsure of his welcome. Skunks are used to people jumping up on things and making loud, strange-sounding noises when they are around. He shyly hung his head. He did so want folks to like him.

Mother smiled in spite of herself. "Isn't he a cute little fellow? My, how he shines. Now, young man, just where do you plan to keep him? There is not room for another thing around here — you know that."

"I thought we could keep him in the orphan box. Your squirrel doesn't stay in it much more."

"I'm keeping two of them," Ralph spoke up, the first chance he had had to utter a word. "And my mother doesn't mind a bit; that is, if I take care of them," he added slowly.

"You hear that, Ronnie?" Mother went on. "Ralph has to take care of his little skunks. Now, see that you do the same with yours."

"You mean I can keep it, if you won't have to take care of it?" Ronnie beamed. For a while he had had his doubts.

"I guess you can. Since when has anything ever left here once it arrived?"

"Daddy's Gila monster eggs — left," Ronnie pointed out as he filled the orphan box with fresh straw and put into it the little animal who was to be known as Little Stinker, regardless.

That afternoon Mother was about to put a plant into the new planter she had recently bought. It was a miniature rocking chair with a small flower pot in place of the customary seat. But she never did plant it. Before she could get back inside with the earth and plant, Little Stinker had discovered the rocking chair and was contentedly rocking back and forth in it. So Mother made a little cushion to cover up the hole, and let him keep it.

By early evening Little Stinker was sitting in his rocking chair, blissfully breaking an egg over Raffle's head.

"There's something wrong outside," said Daddy, jumping to his feet. "Let the dogs out."

Ronnie opened the door and the dogs rushed out. In the distance Ronnie heard Shep and the Gales' dog, Knight. Into the garden and past Timothy Tattercoat rushed a panting deer with a fawn at her heels. She trembled and swayed. The fawn buckled and fell in the new snow.

"It's Lady, your pet doe, Daddy, and her fawn.

Something has been chasing them. She's hurt — her side is bleeding," Ronnie cried. The dogs disappeared, running silently into the forest.

"Yes, but not seriously; it's only a deep scratch, but look!" Daddy lifted her hind leg. "Something has tried to hamstring her!"

There was an ugly wound on her leg.

"What's 'hamstring'?" Ronnie asked, picking the fawn up from the snow. The mother did not mind Ronnie's touching the fawn under these circumstances. She understood.

"To hamstring something means to sever the big muscle in the leg so that the creature cannot run," Daddy explained. "A favorite trick with some predatory animals, especially wolves."

"But they missed, didn't they? She was running in here," Ronnie asked anxiously.

"Yes, had they succeeded, we could have done nothing on earth for this doe, except shoot her. She is more frightened than anything else, I think. Her heart is beating like a trip hammer. Is the fawn all right?"

"There's blood on his back, and a long gash, but he can stand up now," Ronnie answered. "Something sure tried to get them. Now why do you suppose they came to us for help?"

"Because they know us, and trust us. And where

else would they go?"

Suddenly from the forest came the most terrible racket Ronnie had ever heard. It sounded like hundreds of dogs fighting among themselves.

Mother screamed from the doorway. "Lance, here's your gun! Something is killing the dogs! Oh, be careful, but do hurry!"

The noise was fierce. The dogs bellowed as though they were being slaughtered slowly and painfully. Louder and louder grew their cries as Ronnie and Daddy drew near the source.

At first they could see nothing except dogs. They were tangled together, their growls and cries filling the air. They saw their own dogs, Mitzi, Laddie, and Penny, and with them were Shep and Knight. But they were not fighting each other. United, they were tearing at something on the ground, something which snapped and quivered, and then lay still. Blood oozed into the snow.

Ronnie snatched at Mitzi and picked her up. She was so tiny, and so brave. One by one Daddy pulled the other dogs away. There lay a huge gray wolf. He was dead. Ronnie saw in the moonlight that his throat had been torn away. There was blood on the dogs' muzzles, and though they too had suffered wounds, they growled and yelped in victory. Mitzi struggled until she succeeded in freeing herself from Ronnie's arms. She ran to the thicket several yards from the wolf's body, growled and looked back at Ronnie, showing him that something was there. In the thicket lay the body of a second wolf, a smaller one. It was a female.

Daddy lifted one of the big wolf's feet. It was minus a toe. The long reign of Ole Cripple Toe was over. He who had been ruler of the forest for so long now lay still, killed by his domestic brothers.

"There were five against them," Ronnie said. "It wasn't a fair fight."

Daddy looked at Mitzi, who might possibly weigh all of seven pounds. He looked at the other dogs. Then he looked at the wolf, twice as large as any of them.

"It was fair," he answered. "There were two wolves who outweighed them three to one. And you must remember that wolves have a fierce, savage way of fighting. It evened up at about two against two, so don't worry about their not having had a chance. Good dogs!" Daddy said, patting the still growling animals, who had only been doing their duty of protecting Tattercoat Range.

An owl hooted from a tree and flapped across the path of the moon.

"Goodby, old fellow," Daddy said to Ole Cripple Toe. "You've been a gallant foe. I'm sorry to see you go. I hoped that you would stay away from us, and that we would never have to bring you down. But you came too far onto Tattercoat Range, and now you have met your end. I will miss not finding your unmistakable track in faraway places, and hearing your hunting cry on clear moonlit nights."

Ronnie hadn't realized how sad it would be. Daddy was telling one of his wild brothers goodby, just as the Indians used to do. Daddy had loved the wolf, as he loved all forest folk, and had always been glad when Ole Cripple Toe succeeded in eluding the government hunters. Something would be missing from the forests and mountains of Tattercoat Range. One of the guardians of one of the last remaining frontiers of America was gone.

They turned toward his mate. She had died early in the battle. Daddy turned her over, and her dead eyes stared at the moon.

"Oh," Daddy said sadly, just as if the wolf could hear him. "Why didn't you stay away from here and not try to kill our deer? Didn't you know that our dogs would have to kill you if you molested the creatures on the Range? Now, you've left a den of cubs to starve — I'm sorry about that, too."

"How do you know that, Daddy," Ronnie asked.

"She's been nursing puppies," Daddy answered, calling the dogs to him and starting down toward the house.

He washed the blood from the dogs' muzzles, and then sent Shep and Knight home. Looking valiant and pleased, they trotted across the meadow.

"I guess those wolf puppies are miles and miles away," Ronnie mused sadly.

"Not too far," Daddy answered, binding the doe's leg. "The wolves wouldn't hunt too far from their pups. Maybe a mile or so."

"I think I'll hunt for them. They probably will wonder and wonder why their parents don't come back. And they'll whimper and curl up together in little furry bundles until they die," Ronnie said, putting iodine on the fawn's back.

"Not now!" cried Mother. "Not now, at this time of the night, you won't."

"No," Ronnie replied. "But tomorrow Ralph and the dogs and I will hunt them."

"Maybe I will get home in time to help you," Daddy said, leading the doe to the gate. "Go home now, Lady. Your enemy is dead, and you and your fawn are safe. Go home."

The doe looked over her shoulder at them, then

she and the fawn walked slowly toward the thicket, but not as far as their home at the salt lick. Tonight they would stay near the house.

"If you find the pups," asked Mother, not sounding in the least provoked, "what do you think we should do with them?"

"I hadn't thought of that," Ronnie said. "I hadn't thought about anything, except that they're little orphan babies now, and will starve in a lonely den somewhere. I don't know what we will do with them."

"The only thing we can do for them is to take care of them for a little while, then set them free — for they, like Lodge, are true creatures of the wild. We couldn't keep them because they would attack the ranchers' sheep and calves. And we couldn't keep them in a pen." Ronnie had known Daddy would feel this way.

"Well," said Mother softly. "Little Stinker seldom stays in the orphan box any more."

Ronnie and Daddy smiled at her.

Laddie coughed and gagged. Daddy ran his hands over the dog's throat. It was swollen and bruised, and there were tooth marks deep in the flesh.

"You almost got it, fellow! It's a good thing you had the other dogs to help you. That wolf certainly had a good hold on your throat."

"Do you remember what a coward Laddie used to be?" Ronnie asked.

"Never about important things, I guess — He was only afraid of harsh voices, and cruel people." Daddy smiled.

"I think we'll bury Ole Cripple Toe and his mate tomorrow," he went on. "We'll bury them in the pet cemetery. I hate to think of that fallen monarch out there, uncovered."

"Let's not tell anyone he's dead," suggested Ronnie. "If no one knows it, and no one mentions it, maybe we can go right on pretending he isn't gone, and that he's still running in the forest and howling at the moon. 'Spose we could do that?"

"Maybe," said Daddy. "Yes, I think if we tried very hard, we could imagine he is still here."

Ralph and Ronnie, tagged by the dogs, crossed the stream, and started up toward the big pine on the mountainside. Daddy had backtracked the wolves that far. He said that if the puppies were near, they would be someplace in the vicinity of the big pine. Ralph and Ronnie referred to it as the "Lonesome Pine." Even though there were many other pines and evergreens on the mountain, this huge pine seemed to stand alone. The shade spread by its branches discouraged other trees from growing nearby. Its deep, spreading roots had sapped all the strength from the soil, and other small trees that started there died from starvation. Today the jays were scolding from its branches. Daddy often said that jays had probably been scolding from those branches for more than a thousand years.

Up past the chipmunk village they climbed. Ole Cripple Toe's tracks showed plainly in the snow, mingling with the smaller ones of his mate. They searched under every ledge, and under every log, but found no trace of the puppies. Ronnie was growing discouraged, for they would soon have to return home. They would only go a little farther, they decided, for Daddy, when he found that he could not join them, had made them promise not to stay in the forest after sundown.

Penny trotted ahead. She had no idea what the boys were looking for. She merely believed they were on a tramp, as usual. Suddenly she stopped and sniffed the air. Then she circled around an uprooted tree, whining.

From deep in beneath the tree roots, in a safely hidden hole, came an answering whine. But oh, such a feeble little whine. Penny hopped about on stiff legs, barking and clawing at the ground.

Ronnie lay flat on his stomach and turned the beam of his flashlight into the cave-like opening. Small eyes shone in the light, and two tiny creatures huddled far against the back of the lair — two tiny, fat wolf pups. It was impossible for the boys to reach them without removing some of the hard roots and icy snow. That would perhaps take hours.

The scent of the adult wolves was still strong inside. The dogs bristled and growled, remembering the previous night.

"Penny!" Ronnie ordered, pointing to the opening. "Penny, go fetch!"

Penny acted as if she could hardly believe her ears. Surely she hadn't understood correctly. Ronnie never would send her into a wolf den alone. She looked into his face and wagged her tail to show that she forgave him for giving so foolish an order, and that she knew it was only a game. Ronnie pointed again to the opening, and repeated the order. He took her by the scruff of her golden neck and put her head inside the opening.

"Go get them, Penny!" he ordered firmly. "Fetch!"

Penny's heart sank. It wasn't a game. Ronnie really meant her to go into the rank, smelly wolf den. Years of trust and blind obedience finally won.

She crawled slowly inside, looking back at him, for she felt that surely he would countermand the order. Her folks had never sent her into danger before. But the order was not changed. It was, in fact, even more forcibly repeated. Penny crept inside.

Why, there was nothing there at all, in spite of the smell of danger, except two very small pups, who whined happily now and lunged forward in search of a meal. Penny sniffed them, and licked their little faces.

"Fetch, Penny! Bring them here! Gentle, Penny, be gentle!"

Penny looked all around. There was nothing there to fetch. No house slippers, no cigarettes, nothing except a big, well-gnawed bone. Penny looked very carefully, and since there was nothing else to fetch, picked the bone from the earthen floor and wiggled out the opening with it.

"Good dog," said Ronnie, taking the bone, and patting the eager, golden head. "Now, go back, and fetch the puppies, Penny! The puppies, Penny!"

The word "puppy" she understood. Dog-fashion, by the loose skin of its back, she lifted one of the puppies and carried it to Ronnie's outstretched hand. Then, at his insistence, she returned for the other.

"Ralph, they look almost like police-dog puppies!" Ronnie exclaimed.

"Almost exactly!" said Ralph.

The fat little wild babies waddled about on the

ground. Mitzi, who had remained quiet and dignified throughout the rescue operation, although she knew very well that there were babies in that hole, wagged her tail in disbelief. She nosed the puppies, licked them carefully, and cuddled down to warm them. The puppies were disappointed when no lunch was forthcoming. Why, before, when they'd snuggled against a soft furry body, there had been plenty to eat. Mitzi was bewildered. She was trying so hard. The other dogs were watching with interest.

"Ronnie, you'd better not let any of the neighbors know you have these wolf pups," said Ralph, putting the pups into his deep fleece-lined pocket. "The ranchers would be awfully mad if they knew you were raising wolves."

"I know it. We're not to tell anybody," Ronnie added, as they started for home. "We are only going to keep them until they can feed and take care of themselves."

The sun was just casting its last rays upon the mountain when the boys crossed the stream at the otter den.

Daddy arrived home from his errand at the same time.

"Only two puppies?" he was surprised. "Usually wolves have more than that."

Mother had already prepared the orphan box and heated milk.

"It's a good thing there are only two, because they will have to be bottle-fed for quite some time."

"One's a little girl wolf, and one's a little boy," Ronnie announced. "Just like Ole Cripple Toe and his mate. When they grow up we'll hardly know the difference. They'll look just like them, and they'll sound just like them hunting on moonlight nights."

Mother held the bottles very carefully while the puppies drank. Mitzi hopped into the orphan box and cuddled down beside them.

"Mitzi, you nice little dog. Are you going to help me raise them? Are you?" said Mother softly and very kindly, for Mitzi made people feel that way.

Mitzi wagged her tail, and licked the puppies, her black eyes glowing through the thatch of honey-colored hair.

13

MACK, *the Vagabond Dog*

IT WAS a bright, sunny morning, and in Timothy Tattercoat's garden sat a strange dog, larger than any of the O'Learys', wagging his tail in friendly fashion. He had long black hair with white markings, and white feet, but Daddy saw that his coat was matted with burs, and his feet were raw-looking.

"Where did you hail from?" he asked.

The other dogs sniffed in greeting. This was no foe, but a dog like themselves, friendly and gentle, and, in spite of his unkempt appearance, kingly and proud.

"Part shepherd, aren't you?" Daddy mused. "And I'd say, part Husky. You are a beautiful fellow, or will be when the burs are removed. I do know this, that someone has loved you, and has treated you kindly. Are you lost, or have you become one of the wandering tramp dogs, who roam the world? If so, why are you a tramp?"

Though Daddy loved all animals, he loved dogs

most of all. Dogs seemed to know this, and a great number of them made their way to Tattercoat Range, some to remain as Laddie had done, some to have other homes found for them, such as Lazarus, and others to stay but a day or so, and then be on their way.

"Are we going to keep him, Lance?" Mother asked.

"If he wants to stay," Daddy answered. "My, but he's a fine fellow. One of the finest dogs I've ever seen. Look here! The burs under his legs have rubbed him raw, and his feet are sore. He's come a great distance."

They fed him, and he ate politely and with dignity. Then he wagged his tail, and looked gratefully into their faces.

It took a long time to remove the burs, after which he was bathed and brushed. His heavy, thick coat gleamed in black-and-white splendor.

They called him Mack for the gun-shy dog of Mother's childhood, who had also been black-and-white. For a few days he rested, graciously showing his appreciation for the food and kindness he received, and playing happily with the other dogs when his feet got well. Daddy had him immunized against rabies along with the rest of the dogs. Then one day he nuzzled the human members of the family one by one, as if thanking them; and bidding them goodby, he started down the road toward the highway.

Daddy called him back. Almost reluctantly, as if he thought it wouldn't be polite to refuse, Mack turned and trotted back.

Daddy said, "We're not going to try to keep you, for you obviously want to go. But there is something you are searching for, and we will try to help you."

There were always extra collars at Tattercoat Range in case any of the dogs lost his. Daddy got one, then typed a note, folded it carefully in a waterproof covering, and slipped it into a small leather pocket on the collar, and called Mack to him. He fastened the collar around the dog's neck.

He fed the dog again, and looking into Mack's eyes as he scratched his ears said, "Goodby, fellow. I hope you find whatever it is you are searching for."

Daddy loved that dog. It puzzled Ronnie why he let him go.

"I would like to know this dog's history. There is something about him that tugs at one's heart. He is gentle, yet very strong, and there is something so purposeful about him."

"Will we ever see him again? Will he ever come back?" Ronnie asked.

"No, I think that we shall never see him again," Daddy answered softly and regretfully.

The note Daddy had placed in the collar read:

To Whom It May Concern:

I am no beggar, but when I come to you I will probably be hungry, thirsty, and tired, and may need rest for a few days.

Although I do not have a tag, I have been immunized against rabies, on the date above, by Lance O'Leary of Tattercoat Range, who will verify this fact.

I am kind and gentle, and although I was offered a permanent home with the O'Learys, I could not accept, for I am a dog with a purpose.

There is some place I am trying to reach, or perhaps a lost master whom I am trying to find. I know that I must keep searching.

After reading this note, please replace it carefully in the pocket so that the next person may read it too. Although I cannot say a word, I am a grateful fellow, and will appreciate a little food and care, and then, my freedom, to go in search of whatever it is I am trying to find.

For the few days I was a guest at Tattercoat Range I was called Mack, and now answer to that name, although it is only borrowed.

I will show you by my actions how very much I appreciate whatever kindness is shown me on my vagabond journey.

(Signed)   "MACK"
            by LANCE O'LEARY
            Tattercoat Range,
            Colorado

He never came back. This time he reached the highway, turned northward, and trotted along the left-hand side of the road, facing the traffic.

It was almost two years later when the O'Learys received the following letter from Alaska giving them the answer to Mack's determined search:

My dear Mr. O'Leary:

You do not know me — have never heard of me, and yet, I am more grateful to you than to any other person. You once showed a great kindness to my dearest friend. I think that perhaps the letter which you placed in the pocket of the collar about his neck must on several occasions have surely saved his life. This friend is known to you as "Mack," but at birth he was christened "Snow King."

His mother was born in Missouri, where I grew up. She was dear to my heart, as a dog is to a boy who loves her. A beautiful black-and-white shepherd, she had become quite old when I brought her to Alaska with me to homestead. I lived far from people, and she was my constant companion.

She was much too old a dog to have puppies, but I believe all would have been well had she not been caught in a poacher's trap during a raging blizzard. When I discovered her, after hours of searching, her four puppies, part Husky, had just been born. Three of them were dead, but one tiny black-and-white fellow was still alive. I put her and the puppy on a sled and pushed them for two miles through the storm. When we reached home, she lived only long enough to nuzzle once more the puppy whom she had kept alive by the warmth of her own body. Then she feebly licked my hand, and was gone.

I wrapped the puppy, whom I called Snow King, in cotton and a wool sweater, and kept him warm at night by holding him under my arm beneath the covers of my bed. I really had little hope of his living, but how I worked at it, never leaving him, feeding him with warm canned milk every hour. But after nine days his eyes opened, and I knew that I had won the battle.

Snow King was triply dear to me, because of his mother, because of his helplessness — and because he was all I had. For nearly three years we knew the happiest of companionships. Then, for business reasons, I had to return to Missouri, driving through and taking Snow King with me. One night I was unable to find a place where Snow King could stay and had to leave him in the car some distance from my sleeping quarters. Someone broke a window of the locked car and stole him, even though I am sure Snow King put up a great fight. I searched constantly for over a month, and ran ads in all the papers, but couldn't find a trace of him.

Apparently, he managed to escape, or was abandoned by the thieves. The date on your note shows that six months later he was your guest. Written below your signature were the names of other people who helped him. One of them, a year later, had him re-immunized against rabies. These addresses blazed a path to the Northwest, and finally due north.

I am not ashamed to tell you that I cried many times over losing that dog. I had given up hope, and had spent over three hundred dollars, which I could ill afford, in advertisements, but I had made the error of running the ads in papers in the locale where he had disappeared.

After two years, Mr. O'Leary, I was awakened one night three weeks ago by a scratching at the door of my remote cabin — and there was Snow King.

In town last week, I found some tourists who told of having found him by the side of the road in a desolate area, and who brought him in their car for over six hundred miles. So, you see, among other things, he was a hitchhiker too. I believe, however, that if those people had changed their northward course, he would have left them. His unusual sense of direction never failed him, though his feet must often have been torn and tattered. When he was only fifteen miles away from my cabin, he slipped away from the car and came home.

I could not find him, but he found me. His long search is over, and he is no longer a vagabond. But, I cannot force him to get into the car any more. He knows that was how he became separated from me.

I felt that you would be interested in knowing the ending of the story, begun for you two years ago when you fed him, placed the note in his collar, and left him free to continue his search.

Sincerely,
ROD CALVIN

14

OLD-TIMER

Spring had come again and Mother announced early one morning that she intended to go fishing. She invited Daddy too, but he had to get some pictures of the bear cubs and said that he would join her and Ronnie later at the deep pool where Old-Timer, the elusive trout, lived. Daddy gathered his camera, sketch pad, and fishing tackle, and left the house before Mother and Ronnie did.

After Mother had packed the picnic lunch, humming happily, she went into the storeroom where the fishing equipment was kept. Daddy had taken every bit of the good equipment, even the flies.

Undaunted, Mother hunted out a crochet needle, bent it with the pliers, tied a bunch of bantam feathers together as a lure, and cut a length of ordinary twine for her line. Along the way she cut a tough slim sapling to use as a pole.

Bugs followed along beside her. Mother stopped,

stamped her foot, and pointed toward the house. Bugs sat down. Then she got up and stood on her hind legs, patting her forefeet. She even crowed like a rooster. So of course she was allowed to go along.

Before they had gone very far, Mitzi joined them, and tagging along with her were the two wolf pups, eager for their first outing. Mother said they were quite old enough to be allowed to play on the ground. The snow was entirely gone now, and the sun was warm and bright.

Penny and Laddie, who had gone with Daddy, came to join the party when they heard Ronnie's voice.

They reached the place where the pool was formed by the big pine tree lying across the stream. This was Old-Timer's pool and Daddy's favorite fishing place.

Mother arranged herself and her equipment on the bank. She tied the crochet needle on to the twine, and covered it with the wad of bantam feathers.

On hesitant feet, the two little wolves explored the earth and the intriguing forest scents, perhaps dimly remembering their far-off world of two months ago.

Mother's wad of feathers became a soggy mass and sank out of sight. Since she had no reel, she looped the string around her pole, and cast again. The third time she met with success. She tossed the wriggling medium-sized trout onto the bank, removed the hook from its mouth, and put it in the deep grass-lined basket which served as a creel. At almost the same time Ronnie landed his first fish of the day.

Ronnie, however, never took his fishing too seriously, so he decided to eat a sandwich. It had been two whole hours since he had eaten breakfast. He fished lazily, enjoying the woods about him more than the actual fishing.

Laddie and Penny barked and ran toward a scolding squirrel, and Mitzi pricked up her ears with interest at the chipmunk who scampered for one of Ronnie's discarded bread scraps. Daddy usually did not permit the dogs to go fishing with him because they made entirely too much noise. Mother paid no attention to their barks, and did not mind their running around in the least. But then, Mother did not work as seriously at fishing as Daddy did.

Daddy slid down the slope and joined them.

"Poor fishing day," he said in a whisper. "Heavy rains in the streams above. Very poor fishing conditions." He looked at the clouds in the distance. "And you'll never catch any fish that way, honey," he informed Mother kindly. "You're even standing on the wrong side of the bank, with your shadow falling across the water."

"No?" smiled Mother, and went right on plugging

away. "Look in my basket."

Daddy looked at the three big trout which now lay in the basket.

"They are beauties," he said generously. "Now, watch how a real fisherman works. For eight years or more I have been fishing here for Old-Timer. He is invincible, though. No one will ever land him. He'll live to be the great-granddaddy of all trout, free and challenging to the last."

"Are you going to try for Old-Timer today?" Ronnie asked.

"Well, we'll see what happens," Daddy answered, deliberating with great care over his fishing equipment. Fly after fly, hook after hook he discarded until he found the ones that exactly suited the weather conditions. Daddy fished scientifically. At last, the whir of his reel cut the air. Very scientifically, Daddy drew the line to him. He stood on the opposite bank, where no reflection could be cast. When the dogs tried to walk the log to join him, he sent them back. No dogs were going to spoil his fishing.

"Aren't you getting hungry, Daddy?" Ronnie asked. "We brought a big picnic lunch."

"Don't talk!" Daddy remonstrated. "Fish are very susceptible to vibrations."

Mother didn't know about vibrations. She yelled,

"Shoo that chipmunk out of the picnic basket, Ronnie," and cast directly into her shadow.

The wolf puppies were making a great deal of noise, barking happily and chasing each other.

"Golly," said Mother, looping string with all her might, "I've hooked a big one."

Daddy smiled tolerantly. "Probably a root. Don't pull so hard. Give it a steady tug. Now, give a little yank and set the hook in the fish's jaw, in case it *is* a fish, and then pull steadily and firmly."

Mother set her MacGregor jaw, determination written in every line.

"The string is tangled and knotted. I think he's going to yank my arms right out of their sockets."

"Just let him know who's boss, honey. Firmly, now — gently — gently," Daddy cautioned from across the stream.

Mother pulled the line firmly, but not gently, hand over hand with her bare hands. She didn't even realize until later that the line had cut into her flesh. With a furious jerk she flipped her pole, and the trout flew out of the water, through the air, and dangled in a tree above her head, still struggling fiercely, flipping his tail wildly.

Daddy kept calling instructions, but Mother had long ago ceased to hear him. She didn't follow his instructions about untangling the fish scientifically, either. She climbed the tree after it.

"He surely is a big one," she said, removing the hook. "Look, he has six other hooks in his mouth."

Daddy dropped his rod and reel, and leaped over the stream. He gazed at the trout. He looked almost as he had when he lost the Gila monster eggs, as if he were going to burst into tears.

"That," he said almost reverently, "that — is Old-Timer! You landed Old-Timer! What in the world is that you're using for a hook?"

"An old bent crochet hook, and some chicken feathers," Mother answered tranquilly. "You took all the good equipment."

Ronnie stopped eating and looked at Daddy, who sounded as if the world were coming to an end.

"For at least eight years I've tried for that fish with the best equipment money can buy. I've fished scientifically. I've studied the weather conditions and the fisherman's almanac. The almanac says today is a very poor fishing day, and you come down here just because it's a good day for a picnic. You stand on the wrong side of the stream, casting your shadow directly into the water. You get your line tangled, and you don't even have a reel. You snag him in a tree — and you land him. You land him with a bent crochet needle and three chicken feathers!"

Speechlessly, Ronnie pointed to Daddy's expertly designed rod and reel, spinning down the rapids. They were soon lost to sight. Daddy didn't say a word.

Mother was easing the still struggling trout back into the pool. "I've had the fun of landing him and now I will set him free. It is like what you said about Ole Cripple Toe — something would be strangely missing from these streams and mountains if Old-Timer were gone."

After supper Mr. Mallow came to visit.

"I smell fish," he said. "Catch your first string of the season?"

"Well, I didn't," grinned Daddy shamefacedly. "Laurie and Ronnie had good luck, though."

"About time for you to have a try for that big trout Old-Timer, isn't it, Lance?"

"Believe it or not," said Daddy, "that fish has at last met his Waterloo. Laurie landed him today."

"No!" Mr. Mallow exclaimed.

"Coffee?" asked Mother, bringing the tray into the living room and placing it on the coffee table.

"Hear you landed Old-Timer today," Mr. Mallow said to Mother. "That's great! What bait were you using? Flies?"

"No particular bait." Mother flushed.

Daddy laughed. "She caught him with three soggy chicken feathers and a broken-off, bent crochet hook. I've tried everything except that, and always failed."

Ronnie's heart lifted. He had thought Daddy was disgruntled, but he wasn't at all. He had been trying to figure out what he had been doing wrong all the years he had been fishing for Old-Timer. Now he had conceded that Mother had beaten him, and was laughing at the joke on himself. He sounded awfully proud of her, too.

"You were pretty lucky." Mr. Mallow smiled at Mother.

"No," Daddy spoke up. "I've decided that it wasn't just luck. She fooled that fish by fishing for him in a way he didn't know. I've used the most expertly designed equipment, the most scientific methods, and always failed. I don't think Laurie was merely lucky; I think Old-Timer just met a better fisherman than I am. I've always said I'd pin a medal on the fisherman who ever landed him, and that's exactly what I'm going to do."

Daddy was pinning a medal on Mother. Right on her chest, just where a medal should be, Daddy was pinning Trader Horn's cherished, tarnished sheriff's badge.

15

TIMOTHY'S MAGICAL GARDEN

AT BREAKFAST the next morning they talked about returning the wolf pups to the wilderness. Ronnie became silent. He didn't want to take them back. Why, Rack and Ruin were just like any other half-grown puppies, friendly and playful. He wanted them right where they were on Tattercoat Range.

"Why are you so quiet, son?" Daddy asked.

"What if Rack and Ruin don't understand about being wild? What if they starve? They don't even know they're wolves. Like everything else around here, they think they're dogs."

"Once they are back in the wilds they will soon forget about civilization, and their instinct will come to their rescue. They will survive, I assure you, just as Ole Cripple Toe and his mate survived so long. And that is the way we have always planned, remember?"

"Yes, honey," Mother added. "Very soon now they will start straying from Tattercoat Range, and maybe

even killing the ranchers' calves and lambs."

"Well, we could make a pen for them," argued
Ronnie.

"Ronnie," Daddy said firmly. "You know very well
we could do no such thing. Do you remember what
you once said about cages being sad — that you liked
to have our animals running wild and free?"

"I know." Ronnie sighed.

They took Rack and Ruin ten miles up the mountain, found a comfortable den, and left enough food to
last them until they became accustomed to the woods.

The puppies were bewildered at first and found
their way back to the gray house again and again. Even
after they had become adjusted to the wild, they came
down occasionally to romp with the dogs, and wag
their tails dog-fashion at the family who had be-
friended them.

Ronnie was beginning to realize how extensive their
Trailside Museum was. Raffles had built a nest in a
hollow tree not far from the house, and moved in with
his mate. He came to the house every day to visit, and
soon there would be baby coons running all over
Tattercoat Range. Raffles' mate would never come as
far as the house with him, because she could not ac-
custom herself to any other life than that of the wild,

but she did accept the food the O'Learys brought to her, and proved to be as fond of eggs as Raffles was.

Ronnie didn't feel so sad about losing Lodge any more, either. Just the other day they had all gone on a camping trip with Mr. Mallow up into the high peaks so that he could take his annual game poll. They had all suddenly become aware of the thunder of hoofs, vibrating on the stony ground, and just below the spot where they were standing ran a giant elk herd.

The big elk leader sniffed the air and pawed the ground. He had, of course, discovered the people standing above, but since they made no motion toward him or his herd, he led the band slowly along. They grazed as they moved, and remained quite undisturbed as Daddy took pictures and Mr. Mallow made notes for his record.

Toward the rear of the herd, moving in a little band of their own, were several young elk. Though now they were friends, during the rutting or mating season their natures would revert to some basic instinct and they would engage in desperate battles, even to death, for supremacy. One member of this group stopped, sniffed the air, and looked toward Ronnie's party. He put a shy foot forward, almost as though he were feeling his way. Slowly and cautiously he moved toward them, as if he hardly knew what he should do; and at the same time ready to whirl away at a moment's notice. Something seemed to be stirring in the hazy recess of his wild brain, something he remembered.

Daddy grinned and slipped the high-powered binoculars into Ronnie's hand. He looked through them at the young elk. There, clearly through the lenses, could be seen the brand of Tattercoat Range.

"It's Lodge!" whispered Ronnie, handing the binoculars around so that the others could see. "He hasn't forgotten."

"Not quite," Mr. Mallow agreed, "but he would be most reluctant to come with us now, as reluctant as he once was to leave us for the herd."

Slowly, step by careful step, Lodge came toward them, a half-wild, half-tame creature of the forest.

"Lump sugar," whispered Ronnie, fumbling in his big pocket.

He held the lump in his open outstretched hand, hardly moving a muscle.

With hesitation, Lodge came close enough to reach it with his long, soft lips. Then gently, oh, so gently, Ronnie reached out and touched him. Lodge stood for a moment afterward, then, almost as if a silent voice called him back to his kind, he wheeled and with a clatter of hoofs on the rocks, ran swiftly back to the herd.

Ronnie's heart fairly sang with joy. Free elk that he had become, he still remembered. Some small portion of his wild heart had been left on Tattercoat Range — and in Timothy Tattercoat's garden.

And Timothy, standing on his pedestal, neck arched, and forefoot lifted, was always ready to share in the adventures of his forest friends. He loved the wild folk who came to feed and frolic at his feet. He loved the white snow covering the forest with its downy blanket and melting deep into the earth. He loved the happy sunshine that warmed his dappled coat, and spread warmth and light over all the timberland and desert. He loved the birds who followed the warmth of the sun, and who came from the far southland to the great blue-green Rocky Mountains in the spring. Thousands and thousands of them lived at Tattercoat Range, and in the great national forests surrounding it. Best of all, though, he loved the birds who remained with him through the winter, and sang their cheery songs even when food was scarce and the weather cold. Timothy's magic had its effect on these wild creatures too. Even the quarrelsome bluejays had come under his spell. Ronnie recalled the day he had seen several jays flitting about the garden carrying food to another bird. He knew that it was too early in the season for them to be feeding their young, and then he saw that it was not a baby bird they were feeding, but a full-grown one. The bird was sitting on the ground beside one of the blue-spruce trees. He was pathetically patient, not noisy and shrill like the rest; and not one, but five birds fluttered about him, carrying crumbs from the feeding station. Ronny got the binoculars for a closer look, and saw why the other birds were helping this one. The bluejay's lower beak had been broken off, making it impossible for him to pick up and swallow the food. So, one by one, the other jays were bringing food and placing it inside the injured bird's mouth.

And now the moon was coming up, big, round and full. In the garden a strange thing happened. Timothy Tattercoat's jet-glass eyes sparkled, and the chickadees fluttered sleepily on his back. Then suddenly, he slowly and happily winked at the man in the moon, and the man in the moon winked back — perhaps because a new occupant had just moved into the orphan box.